Deck This House

Ivy Beck

Contents

Chapter One

Living in freaking Tinsel, Tennessee in the heart of the Christmas season was going to be the death of him.

Reindeer, both plastic and real, giant blowup snowmen, decorated Christmas trees in front yards, and lights upon lights adorned every house in town. The businesses downtown were not spared in the massacre. Garland and bows, wreaths and ribbons covered every store window.

The snow added to the ambiance. Blanketing everything in white, reflecting all those nauseating lights, causing everything to glow even more.

Gabe had never seen anything quite like this. Probably because he'd lived the last twenty years on military bases, or overseas where everything was the same color—mud brown. He felt like he needed to put his sunglasses on to drive through town even though it was past sundown. The windows on his truck were tinted but it didn't matter. The wattage was spectacular. And he didn't mean that in a positive sense. It was over the top, ridiculous even. These people's power bills must be through the roof.

Moving here just over six months ago, this was his first time experiencing all this madness. Nobody had warned him. But then again with the name Tinsel he should have guessed. Plus, most people saw this as a positive thing. Christmas was a special time. A time to decorate with lights and all the trimmings. To sing and laugh. To eat, drink and be merry.

But to him it was a time that he'd rather forget.

He wished they could skip through the calendar from the day after Thanksgiving to New Year's Day. He hated Christmas. And living here now, he was so screwed. All the excessive joy only pissed him off even more. Just call him the Grinch.

Turning down his street, Gabe yawned. The meeting with his lawyer had taken longer than he'd planned. Plus, they'd met at his office in Nashville, so he'd been on the road a while.

Gabe was pleased with how fast things were moving along with his plan to buy out a local businessman who was ready to hand his business over to someone else.

Amos Tucker had been training and issuing personal pilot's licenses for over thirty years now and he was ready to retire.

Gabe had been trained by the best, qualifying right alongside Navy Pilots, then furthering his career in the Marines providing air support to ground troops, conducting recon missions, and even had a few opportunities over his career to engage in air-to-air combat.

The idea of flying as his retirement job was the best thing he could think of. It wasn't like he was going to take up golfing now that he'd put in his twenty years of service. He sucked at golf. Staying busy was important to him, and flying was one of his favorite things to do.

He'd made a date to take his grandpa up with him tomorrow. His grandpa had never flown before, so he'd have to make it a memorable experience. He just wished he had more memorable experiences with him to reflect on, but he'd only learned that he had a grandfather last year.

Gabe had been in Afghanistan when he'd received an email from a man named Joseph Shepherd. The first name wasn't familiar, but the last name was. A tingling sensation had filled his fingers when he'd clicked on the name.

A short letter followed. He'd introduced himself and got right to the point.

Joseph's daughter was Gabe's mother.

A mother who had died on Gabe's tenth birthday. A mother who had done her best, but it had never been consistent enough or good enough to keep them well fed or in adequate shelter for very long. She'd never mentioned her family.

He'd never asked. At least, not out loud. He'd wondered though. They'd moved around a lot, never allowing him to form any strong friendships. He mostly kept to himself and tried not to take up too much space.

Gabe had stared at that email for nearly ten minutes. His mind whirring with all the possibilities and all the questions that his younger self had always wanted to ask.

Now here they were one year later.

He'd retired from the Marines and rented a small house in a quiet neighborhood on the other side of town from his grandpa. Wanting to be close, but also wanting to give them both space, without making any permanent decisions.

He had no idea how to be a grandson.

Gabe let out another yawn, longer and louder this time. He hadn't quite figured out this whole sleeping thing now that he was stateside. He'd been more into taking combat naps while on duty, since he always felt the hum from being "on." Coming off that high had been a hard go. He was starting to adjust, but the sleeping-through-the-night thing was slow going. He slept when he could and fueled up on black coffee the rest of the time.

Oh, and exercise. He ran at least five miles a day. In sun, rain or snow. Inclement weather didn't scare him. Routine kept him sane. He needed that time to decompress each morning after the nightmares that usually plagued what little sleep he did get.

And speaking of snow, he wasn't a huge fan. He'd lived in North Carolina at Camp Lejeune for many years and only saw snow there once. They were so close to the ocean that the temps rarely dropped enough for a snowfall.

The snow was really falling now. It was forecasted to drop at least two inches. Turning down his driveway, Gabe had to blink at what he saw before him. The heavy flakes covered his windshield and Gabe hit the wipers, upping their speed.

"What the hell is this?" he grumbled, his voice loud in the enclosed cab.

Gabe put the truck in reverse and backed it up to the street. Maybe he was at the wrong house. Nope. That was his mailbox, and this was indeed his house. It should have been a small, dark house with only the porchlight left on for security.

But right now, what he was seeing confused the hell out of him.

The entire structure plus the yard was decked out in Christmas.

It was literally like elves had thrown up all their Christmasy joy right there on his property. His head swiveled to the left and right. All his neighbors had their homes decorated, but this was outrageous.

This was borderline comical.

This was a mistake.

Gabe slowly inched forward along the driveway and threw the gear into park. He couldn't

"What's the address you're calling about?" The woman's voice now sounded strained and a lot less joyful. Bah humbug. He gave her his address then heard the clicking of keys on a keyboard. "Oh, I see. Yes, I just finished decorating that property about two hours ago." She paused and he heard more keyboard clicks. "Wait, you don't like it?"

Gabe closed his eyes and rubbed his fingers along the sides of his nose, shifting the sunglasses up off his eyes. His headache was spreading.

"Are you Gabriel Shepherd?" Then more silence while she likely read something on her computer. "I have here that you called last week and ordered the 'Full Monty.'"

Momentarily distracted by the woman's voice, he had to shake his head to clear it before he blurted, "What the hell is that?"

"The Full Monty? It's the works, the whole shebang, the whole kit and caboodle—"

"Okay, stop. Sorry." Gabe paced to the edge of his porch and turned back, scuffing up his snowy footprints. "I am Gabriel Shepherd. Gabe, actually," he grumbled. Gabe ran a hand across his head, disrupting the short hairs on top, leaving them standing straight up. "But I didn't order anything. I don't even like Christmas," he confessed, his voice trailing off as he noticed a bright neon star over his front door.

Her gasp was loud in the silence of the night surrounding him. Then the train horn honked and he gritted his teeth.

"Look, it's all right for other people to celebrate. You do you and all that. But leave me out of it," he muttered and punched the back of the snowman's head. The inflatable bobbed forward, bumping into the reindeer beside it. "So when can you come take all this down?" Gabe heard another gasp. Guess that was the first time she'd ever heard that.

"Oh, I'm sorry. We have a strict policy that once decorations are in place, they have to remain for at least three weeks. We are so busy putting them up all around town that we don't have room on the books for a take-down. Not until after Christmas."

Not until after Christmas.

Those words echoed in his head. How the hell could he stand living in this gingerbread house for three more weeks like this? Well, one thing he could do was unplug the lights immediately. He marched over to where a bank of wires was plugged into a power strip. He yanked the plug from the outlet on the porch and the blazing midnight sunlight blinked out in an instant. Back to pitch darkness. Just like he liked it.

"I'll be counting down the days until then."

"I'm so sorry for the misunderstanding. I don't know how it could have happened." Gabe could hear the confusion in her tone. "I have your name and address down, requesting I decorate today."

Gabe watched as the inflatables slowly deflated, the air inside sizzling out. "Wait. Who paid for this? Do you have a record of payment?"

"Hold on. Let me look." He could hear more typing on a keyboard. Then a mouse click. Another. "I have down that a Ryan Blaylock paid with his Master Card."

Ryan, you sonofabitch! "Well, that explains it. Thank you for your time."

"I hope you can find some joy in what I put up for you, Mr. Shepherd," she said quickly, thinking maybe that he was going to hang up on her. "I always find the lights and all the colors bring a smile to my face."

Yeah, not happening. But he did realize that something—her voice, even though it dripped sunshine and candy canes—had caused his lips to curve a little. Most people wouldn't describe it as a smile, but he noticed the difference. "What's your name? I missed it earlier."

"Holly. Holly Noelle." There was silence on his end. Wow...who would do that to their child? "Yep," she continued, a soft chuckle in her voice, "you guessed it. My parents LOVE Christmas. My dad is actually the town Santa. Maybe you've seen him in the park posing for pictures with all the kids."

"Uh, no." He cleared his throat. "I haven't been in town that long. I just moved here in the summer, so I wasn't prepared for...all this." Why was he telling a complete stranger this. *Hang up, you moron.* Before she could comment on his oversharing, he quickly ended the conversation with, "Thanks again for clearing up this mess for me. I'll have to personally *thank* Ryan Blaylock for this. Have a good night."

HOLLY DIDN'T THINK she'd want to be thanked in the way that Gabriel Shepherd was implying. Sounded more like a whooping. Or a beat down. Someone was grumpy. *Makes me wonder why.* What could happen to a person that caused them to hate Christmas?

Not just *not like it*, but to be *angry* over a friend who obviously surprised them with full-on house and lawn decorations for Christmas.

She knew her business brought joy to people. He was an anomaly. Holly didn't usually allow other people's emotions to direct her own if she could help it. She shook her shoulders and let his sour mood slide right off her. Making her way from what she affectionately called her home office, which really was the breakfast nook off the kitchen where she kept her laptop set up, she padded in her elf slippers to her bathroom. She needed a long soak in the bath tonight after spending hours up on Mr. Grumpypants' roof.

The snow had started coming down this afternoon while she and her younger sister Caroline attached all the festive bulbs along the contours of his roof. The first snowfall of the year was so magical. Here in eastern Tennessee, they were lucky enough to experience all four seasons in this neck of the woods of the Smoky Mountains.

And right now, they were in full-on winter, even if it was a few days before the calendar said so.

Turning on the water, she let the tub fill, adding in Snickerdoodle bath bubbles, her favorite for this time of year. Smelling it made her want to eat a bunch of cookies and drink hot chocolate.

Oh! Don't mind if I do! She never turned down the offer of hot chocolate, even if it was she who had suggested it.

On her way to the kitchen, Holly averted her gaze from the sad, bare evergreen planted in a pot in her living room. The unopened tubs of ornaments mocked her as she stepped around them.

She felt the dichotomy down to her soul.

On the outside, her house was decked out completely since that was her business after all. But inside, she'd only had time to buy her tree and get the tubs of decorations down from the attic.

Her house reflected her in a lot of ways. She too was decorated on the outside. Bubbly, happy, Holly Jolly personality with all the trimmings. But inside...inside, she just wasn't feeling it this Christmas. For the first time ever, she had more Ebeneezer Scrooge than Buddy the Elf running through her veins.

She still had the holiday spirit inside. It just wasn't as loud as it had been in years past.

Holly set the kettle on the stove for hot water. Pulling the reindeer mug off the shelf, she hoped that Rudy would help put her in a better mood. Scooping cocoa powder out of the tub, she doctored up her mug while the water was boiling. She grabbed a bowl and tossed in two fresh snickerdoodle cookies that her mom had made this morning.

From the smart speaker on the counter beside her Nat King Cole's deep baritone wished her a Merry Christmas. His words brought to mind the conversation she'd just had with Gabriel Shepherd. Because her heart hurt for the man, she tossed another cookie in the bowl.

The name Gabriel Shepherd wasn't familiar to her. She knew a Joseph Shepherd. He was friends with her grandfather. They both worked at the Chevrolet Plant together until they retired. But as far as she knew Joseph didn't have any family in the area.

Maybe Gabriel just shared the last name, and he was completely unrelated.

Holly poured the steaming water into her reindeer mug and stirred it with a peppermint stick. It was the only way to drink hot chocolate, she thought with a grin as she brought the mug to her mouth. Blowing across the top, she gingerly took a sip between the antlers.

"Ahhh, just right."

Thoughts of Gabriel followed her as she climbed into the bath. Holly pulled her long hair up into a sloppy bun on top of her head as she sunk below the bubbles. The sound of his voice hadn't given away his age. But one thing she had noticed—his deep voice and all the grumbling he'd done had made a small tingle, that started deep in her belly, get hotter, morphing into something more like dripping honey as it coursed throughout her veins.

Holly lifted a hand covered in bubbles and fanned her face. "Lord, it's getting hot in here." Determined to relax in her bubble bath she wiped her hand on a towel and tapped her tablet on. Clicking the Hallmark Channel app, she geared up the next one in the lineup and settled in for a long soak with her favorite movies and snacks.

Now if only she could get his voice out of her head, she could get on with that relaxing bit.

Chapter Two

Gabe leaned back against his closed front door and sighed. Ryan was gonna get his ass kicked for this. If only he was stateside. But Ryan was finishing up a deployment in Afghanistan and Gabe didn't know when he'd get to see him next.

His mouth moved into a mischievous grin when he dialed Ryan's number. Putting it on speaker, he moved to the kitchen. He was gonna need a beer for this conversation. He was just reaching in the fridge when a grumpy voice croaked through the open line.

"Do you know what time it is?"

Gabe popped the top and chuckled. "As a matter of fact, I do."

"Why the hell are you calling me then? I just got to sleep—" Ryan paused, presumably looking at his watch, "shit, only an hour ago. This better be good."

"Oh, it's good all right. Too bad I unplugged everything, or I'd take you on a video chat tour of my front yard. Even though the sun has already set it looked bright as mid-day when I got home ten minutes ago."

That was met with silence.

"Aren't you curious why?"

More silence. And a throat clearing. "Guess you're not cool with getting punked then. I told the guys you'd hate it. Like, not just be annoyed by it, but actually hate it."

He was right. "So why the hell did you do it?"

"It was our retirement gift to you."

"I retired six months ago."

"But it wasn't Christmas then. We just knew you were always annoyed by Christmas and all the trimmings. We did it in fun. No harm, no foul." Gabe could hear rustling in the back-ground, like Ryan was sitting up or getting out of bed. "Why is that?"

This time he offered silence in reply. But he caved. "I've got my reasons."

"I know, man, and I've known you for ten years. I've gone to battle with you. Cleaned up your bloody wounds. And I still don't know those reasons."

"It's because they're personal."

"Didn't you hear the part about cleaning your bloody wounds?" Ryan's voice rose with emo-tion. "That's pretty personal if you ask me."

Yeah, it was. He trusted Ryan with his life. Just not with his past. He didn't share that part of himself with anyone. He'd always changed the subject whenever family history came up. Ryan knew Gabe's mother died and he didn't have anyone else, but that was the extent of it.

"Look, man, I'm sorry," Ryan groveled. "The guys put me up to it. If only I had access to your door video cam, I'd have loved to have seen your face." Ryan's laugh made Gabe roll his eyes. He'd been privy to many pranks by Ryan over the years. He'd sat by and watched his friend pull shit on all the other guys too. He was quite the trickster. But he had a good heart.

"It was a helluva face all right," Gabe griped. He knew Ryan had done it out of fun, but he was feeling overwhelmed with it all. It was enough seeing it all over town and outside each of his windows. But to have all that Christmas mumbo-jumbo spilling out all over his yard and dripping from his house was just too much.

"Can't you call and get them to take it down? But, wait, take a pic of it first," he added quickly. "We wanna see it."

Gabe grunted. "I already called. The moment I stepped foot on my porch." Gabe took a swallow of beer when his mind drifted to the sound of Holly's voice. "Holly—the woman I spoke to—said it's their company policy that the decorations have to stay up for three weeks. They're too busy to come back any sooner to remove them." There he was grumbling again. He wasn't sure when that had started, but it likely coincided with the first decoration that went up in the park downtown. And that had been on the first day of November. What happened to the turkey month? Shouldn't they only be thinking about Thanksgiving in the month of November?

Nope. Not this town. Once he saw that first set of garland draping around the gazebo, it was like a fast-spreading rash all over the town. Next came wreaths on doors, ribbons circling light poles, ornaments being placed on the evergreens in the park.

By mid-November it had spread to pandemic proportions.

"Good, then I'll get to see them after all."

Gabe paused his hand halfway to his mouth. He'd been about to take another sip. "Huh? What do you mean?"

"Cheryl left me."

Those words came out in the saddest tone he'd ever heard from Ryan Blaylock's mouth. The man was forecasted to be ninety-nine percent sunshine most days. Gabe set the beer down and scrubbed a hand over his face, scraping across the growth that had accumulated since this morning.

"I'm sorry, Ryan." He didn't know what else to say. Relationships for them were hard. Frequent deployments. Gone for weeks at a time. Not really being able to share with your significant other where you were. Or if you were safe. Any type of relationship they ever had was often strained. Cheryl and Ryan had been together for nearly a year now, having met when they'd been stateside for a large chunk of time. Gabe had been hopeful for his friend, but the odds were just stacked against them.

Ryan's sigh broke into his thoughts. "Yeah, me too."

"Are you thinking of coming here?"

"If you'll have me."

Gabe didn't hesitate. "You're welcome anytime. Just know I don't do anything special for this time of year. I tend to hunker down and wait for it to pass."

Kinda like a tornado.

***

"What shift am I working tomorrow night?"

Holly rolled her eyes and flopped back on her bed, tucking her phone against her ear. Her youngest sister Bella was the least responsible of all of them. She was barely an adult and it showed most of the time. "You don't work tomorrow night. You're working with Chris on Thursday. We went over this at the meeting this morning. Weren't you listening? I thought I saw you adding things to your calendar."

"Oh, yeah, I was. I forgot to put my waxing appt in for next week. Seeing the calendar reminded me."

Holly felt another eye-roll coming on. "Maybe add your shift times to your calendar as well so you'll be prepared and not have to call me to ask."

"I like calling you."

"And I like talking to you. But you're an adult now, sweet sister, so you need to come up with a way to manage your schedule. Especially around all your college classes. I'm sure your cell phone has an excellent calendar with reminders. I use mine all the time." Like tonight, she'd added a note to follow up with Gabriel Shepherd to see if the merriment she'd put up had cheered him up yet.

Or if he was ready to rip it all down.

Holly shifted against her pillows and switched the phone to her other ear. Tucking the robe tighter across her chest, she crossed her slippered feet at the edge of her bed.

"Are you working tomorrow?"

"Yes, I'm working with Eve. Mom might need help with the set up, so I'll likely be there early."

Bella snorted. "That's cuz you have the first-child syndrome. I've heard it's rough."

Holly rolled her eyes. "Nice, sassy."

"Maybe there'll be a cure for it someday," she mocked.

"And she just keeps going," Holly mumbled around the grin her lips couldn't help but form.

"Night-night, Holly Jolly," Bella said in a sing-songy voice. "See you soon."

Maybe there'll be a cure for it someday.

Maybe. Holly hung up and closed her eyes. She dropped the phone and scrubbed her hands down her face in frustration. *If only.* If only she didn't volunteer for everything. If only she didn't feel responsible for her younger siblings all the time. Always helping them out, guiding them, leading them. Always being all that she can be.

Wow, she sounded like a commercial for the Army.

"Ugh," Holly groaned and forced herself to get up and stop wallowing.

She really did feel like she was getting stretched a little too thin lately. The holiday event schedule was packed, but they did live in Tinsel, Tennessee. People took the spirit of Christmas and celebrating the season seriously here.

Being an elf and helping the children have a magical time was one of her favorite things to do. And now she had her own business which thankfully happened mostly during the daylight hours, whereas the Santa's Village events occurred in the evening.

But that didn't leave much time for herself this time of year.

"But wait, there's more," she grumbled aloud as she reentered her bathroom to slather her body with lotion. It was gingerbread scented and she was in love with it. Sniffing the bottle she closed her eyes. *And I really should stop talking to myself out loud!* That was a side effect of living alone. She didn't even have a cat or a goldfish to pretend to be having a conversation with.

The *more* part involved her full-time, year-round job, which was doing the accounting for her family's roofing business. She'd started out as grunt labor up on the roofs when she was a teenager, like her brother did now. Thankfully, it hadn't taken long until she'd worked her way off the roof and inside the office. Her accounting degree helped. Numbers were her thing and she loved that job too.

Holly realized she had a problem.

She took on too many things.

Her Christmas lighting biz only took place from November to mid-January, so she wasn't this busy all year round. But this time of year tended to be busy anyway for a regular person, she just tripled her workload by starting this new business. It all stemmed from helping her neighbor put up her lights last year. Miss Trudy suggested she go into business doing it, that more people like her would love to decorate, they just couldn't get up on a ladder to do it. *"You're really good at this. Plus, you aren't afraid to be up on the rooftops. Now, me, I'd fall rump over tea kettle if I tried,"* she'd said with a cackle.

She released a heavy sigh and tugged open the top drawer of the vanity. She set out the jars of creams and started opening the lids. Dabbing on the eye serum first, she paused to take in her face. At thirty-two years old her skin was still tight with only a few wrinkles. Avoiding those, she focused on her eyes.

They were a bright blue and her favorite feature. She was the only one of her siblings to have her mother's eyes. The others all had hazel eyes like their father. Holly was proud of her baby blues. Tonight, though, her eyes were not as bright as usual. That probably had a lot to do with how tired she was.

Working so hard left little to no time for fun. She hadn't hung out with her friends in ages, definitely not since Halloween. It was like once the stroke of midnight happened ending Halloween that it suddenly became the Christmas season here. And she immediately got to work. If she wasn't out decorating houses already, she was in planning meetings for putting Santa's Village together.

Another sad fact—her last date. She couldn't remember when it was or with who. Holly closed her eyes and rubbed her temples.

She never thought she'd get to thirty-two without ever having a serious relationship. Serious as in, thoughts about marriage. She'd dated. She'd had long-term relationships. But never any boyfriends that she included in family events. Not a single one of her past boyfriends would have ever dressed as an elf and helped out in Santa's Village.

On second thought, that was probably asking a lot of just about anyone.

Holly added collagen cream to the rest of her face and neck. It was high time she started living for herself. She needed to learn to say no to some things, and to say yes to more things that involved meeting someone. Maybe this year her Christmas wish should be to find someone who lit up her world and made her heart sing.

Holly found it funny that a certain someone came to mind immediately. He had a sexy voice, but a grumpy attitude.

How could anyone hate Christmas?

Chapter Three

Gabe placed his empty coffee mug in the top rack of the dishwasher. Grabbing his beanie off the island and a single house key, he headed to the front door. He tucked the key into the inside pocket of his shorts and zipped up his outer layer. Even though it was winter, he only ever ran in shorts. Doubling up layers on his top half helped keep his core warm, but he needed to have his legs free to move. The addition of the beanie was only because it was still snowing.

Gabe dreaded walking out the front door.

His heart pounded and he had to shake his head.

He was a Marine for God's sake. This was getting ridiculous. He was going to have to come to terms with the over-the-top celebration of the season now that he lived here. He could ignore what was in his front yard. At least he wouldn't have to see all the glowing lights this time. And the blowups would just be puddles of material lying in the snow.

Shaking off the dread he opened his door.

Then stepped back when he saw a woman standing there, hand raised to knock. Her startled face said she wasn't expecting him either. "Oh, I'm sorry. I was just about to knock."

Gabe recognized her voice instantly.

He drew in a breath to calm his racing heart. Not from the surprise of someone on his porch, but from her stunning beauty. Her blue eyes drew him in immediately. His lips twitched when her gaze lowered to take in his exposed legs. His eyes followed the movement of her throat when she swallowed hard before raising her eyes back to his.

Her long dark hair hung straight below her wine-colored beanie, falling across the shoulders of her puffer jacket of the same color, resting on top of the *Deck This House* logo on her chest.

"Hi."

"Hi," she echoed. Then he was nearly knocked breathless when twin divots popped out of her rosy cheeks next to her blazingly white smile. "Hi, I'm Holly Noelle from *Deck This House*. We spoke on the phone last night. I could hardly sleep worrying about how upset you were with the decorations." Her voice appeared to have lost all the cheeriness he'd first heard when she'd answered the phone last night. He hated that his grumpy attitude had affected this ball of sunshine.

"I'm Gabe." He remembered his manners, beaten into him twenty years ago when he stood in formation with all the other recruits in his battalion. "Nice to meet you." Gabe held out his hand. She quickly pulled off her glove and reached for his. Her skin felt soft and warm against his rough palm. The moment his fingers enveloped her whole hand he felt heat shoot up his arm. Her eyes widened upon contact.

Did she feel it too?

Holly cleared her throat when she dropped her hand. "Nice to meet you too."

Gabe suddenly remembered why she was there and said, "You didn't have to come by. I'm sorry if I came across as gruff last night. I was just in shock. I'd never—this was more—"

"Than you'd ever imagined?" she asked with a chuckle, her dimples winking at him.

Man, that heat he'd felt on contact danced along his nerves following that chuckle.

Gabe nodded his head, unable to speak.

Holly stood up straighter, her boots shifting on the wood planks below her feet. "I wanted to let you know that I was able to tweak the sched-ule, and I can work you in for a take-down—"

Gabe raised his hands in surrender, waving his palms back and forth, still gripping the beanie in his left hand. "That's not necessary. I hope you can undo any changes you made to the schedule for me. I'm not going to let this bother me. And I certainly don't want to put you out."

Holly shook her head, her hair sliding across the slickness of her jacket. "I don't ever want a client to be unhappy. And if you aren't satisfied with the job I did, I want to make it right."

Gabe pointed to his yard. "But this wasn't your fault. You did your job. It just wasn't a job I asked for."

Holly shuffled her feet again, dropping her head to half-hide her grin. "So, how did your friend react when you thanked him?" she asked, emphasizing *thanked*.

Gabe couldn't help his own chuckle, irrationally pleased that she remembered their conversation from last night. "He was a little pissed at me for calling when I did. It was the middle of the night in Afghanistan."

"Is he in the military?" She paused, her head tilting with her inspection of him. "Are you in the military?"

"Yes, he is." He nodded. "And I'm retired as of this summer." He saw her looking over his hair style. The high and tight was typically a dead giveaway for any military man. Even though he could do something else with it these last six months it was habit at this point. He went every week to the barber in town to keep it up.

"Oh, well, thank you for your service." She smiled at him. Even though he was prepared for her dimples, they still hit him like a punch to the gut.

Gabe nodded. He always felt uncomfortable when people said that phrase. Like it was just a line. But he understood why people said it. And he appreciated their gratitude. There wasn't enough of it from people these days. Being in the military was hard and most people didn't do it for thanks. They did it out of a sense of pride and honor for the country they love.

He'd done it because he'd aged out of foster care and had nowhere to go. So he'd enlisted. He'd desperately wanted a family, a brother-hood, and he'd earned it, as well as strengthen-ing that pride and honor for his country along the way.

"Do you have family here in town?" she asked then rubbed her hands together. What was he doing keeping her out in the cold like this? Gabe looked beyond her at the light snow still falling.

Pointing to the room behind him, he apolo-gized, "I'm sorry, would you like to come in?"

Holly shook her head and waved him off. She also slipped her glove back on. "No, no. You were headed out." Her gaze dropped once again to his shorts and exposed legs. Did he see a little admiration there? He'd always been fit and told that he had kick-ass legs, with his calves taking the prize. "I have an appointment anyway. I just wanted to stop by and talk to you in person. I don't want any unhappy customers. They can kill a business these days, you know," she added with a forced chuckle. Holly stepped back to-wards the edge of the porch. "I'll check back in on you to make sure you don't want to take me up on that opening for a take-down. Nice to meet you, Gabe." She paused a few seconds after her last words. Her eyes seemed to rove over his face, causing his skin to heat up. Her lips curved into a smile, but not one big enough to flash her complete dimples, just a hint.

"Same, Holly." He watched her walk down his porch steps, admiring the tight fit of her cargo pants. "Have a good day," he called out when she was on the sidewalk leading to the truck parked behind his. A magnet on the side door showed her logo. A couple of ladders and tubs were stacked in the truck bed.

Guess she was off to make someone else's day bright and jolly.

Bah humbug.

But Gabe had to admit he wasn't feeling as down as he had ten minutes ago. He'd never say he was feeling bright and jolly, ever. But her smile and dimples had made his heart beat faster. Gabe waved from the porch steps when she honked at the end of the driveway. She must have hated seeing all her work turned off and deflated in the snow.

He was such a jackass.

It wasn't her fault.

He couldn't even blame Ryan. But he wanted to.

It was his own damn fault. He needed to move on and get over his past. It was long gone, over thirty years ago. Maybe moving here was what he needed. To have the thing that he most hated thrown in his face like this. To be surrounded by all the sappy, sickeningly sweet, Christmas cheer and not let it make him want to bury his head in the sand and wait for January.

Gabe pulled the beanie on his head and jogged off the porch, heading west through the neighborhood, keeping his eyes front and center so he didn't let the Christmas chaos get him down.

***

Holly drew her lips into her mouth on the way back to her truck. *Wowza.* That man had legs for days. Tanned and hairy with muscles galore. He was certainly fit. And he was obviously headed out for a run now.

In the snow.

Wearing shorts.

She'd taken the time to stretch a little between rolling out of bed and donning her not-so-sexy long johns before layering up, then grabbing her bagel and coffee to go this morning. That was it. No yoga. No treadmill. Well, she didn't have one of those, so that was a given. But to go out and run in this was madness. Guess he was dedicated.

Hopping in the truck, she looked back at the sad house with her friends lying flat on the snow. Gabe's actions didn't seem to match his words. If he was okay with the decorations, then why were they unplugged? She hadn't been able to help the frown that had curved her lips when she'd pulled in the drive. Frosty, the

Yeti, Rudy and the train all looked so sad lying in the snow.

She loved blowups, like most people, putting them up for all the holidays. He'd never know how strong the pull was to dash over and rescue them. She'd fought it, but these guys deserved better. Hopefully, he'd change his mind and plug them back in.

Holly honked at the end of the driveway and waved.

Now, the next person's house she was scheduled to deck out had rented ten inflatables for her yard. They must be kindred souls.

Pulling up to the house, Holly was surprised to see Chris leaning against the front porch rail. What was he doing here? Didn't he have school? She didn't want to blast him with questions because she knew her brother was struggling. High school was hard to begin with. But being more on the nerdy side he was having a rough go of it.

"Morning, Kris Kringle," she greeted after shutting her driver's door. "I didn't have you on the schedule today."

Chris pushed himself off the rail and stood at his full height, four inches taller than her. He was gangly, thin and his head looked too big for his body, but he was starting to fill out. He'd shot up those four inches practically overnight.

"It's a teacher workday," he said in response. His voice had been changing as well and she hoped it would make the full transition soon, giving him one less thing to stress about.

"Uh huh."

Chris turned his hazel eyes on her and adamantly said, "It is, I promise. I'm not skipping."

What could she do but believe him? She shrugged it off. "Well, good. I could use some extra hands today since I've got another setup to do right after this one."

Chris joined her at the truck and started removing the ladders, carrying them up to the house. Holly unloaded the tubs and started pulling out the blowups. She took a moment to knock on the front door to see if Janet was home. She got no answer, so she continued on with her task. She liked to let the homeowners know she was getting on their roof so they wouldn't be startled from inside.

Holly pulled out her clipboard and shuffled papers around until she found the design format. Placing it on top, she called Chris over. "So here's the layout," she said holding the clipboard so he could see. "All the blowups will go here and here. We're going to put lights in that tree," she said, pointing with her pencil at the Maple in front of her. "And along the porch railing, front windows, and the roof. She wants icicles to hang along the gutters. Which job do you want to start with?"

Chris grinned and said, "Blowups."

Holly bopped him on the head with her clipboard and headed back to the truck to get some brooms. The snow was beginning to taper off but a couple of inches covered the roof. She needed to remove it so she could get her lights attached.

Holly stopped at the sidewalk before coming back to the house. She paused to take it all in, easily seeing what it would look like after it was all decorated. She visually assessed where the end of the lights needed to be set and how many power strips she was going to need.

Charging over the snow-covered grass, Holly set to work. After stationing the ladders where she wanted them, she carried a broom up one to get started on clearing off the roof. Luckily for her, she didn't have any effects of heights. No vertigo, no fears about falling. She'd always felt pretty easy up on a rooftop. Even one covered in snow. She'd worn her extra-grippy boots today to counter that.

The snow was so soft that it didn't want to move around much with the bristles, so she knelt down and used the pole end of the broom to sweep the powder off the shingles. She had the design for the lights memorized so she only put her effort into the sections where she needed to attach the stringers to the shingles. More snow was predicted, and winter officially started tomorrow.

Feeling around her waist Holly searched for her tape measure. She'd thought she'd clipped it on when she was last at the truck. Glancing down she saw Chris standing in the yard, his fist choking a deflated Frosty glaring at the phone in his other hand. Uh oh. He looked mad.

"Hey, Kris Kringle!" He didn't even look up. So she tried again. "Chrissy! I need your help." That got his attention. He hated being called Chrissy.

Chris looked up, his glare now directed at her. "What?"

"Can you get my tape measure for me, please? It's in the truck."

She watched him release a long sigh as he headed to the truck. She never knew if she should just come out and ask him what's bothering him, or let it go. Hopefully, she could get him to share with her and she wouldn't have to seem like she was prying. Chris returned to the deflated inflatables that he'd left in a pile. He looked like he was about to throw the tape measure up to her.

"No throwing! I don't want to slip on this snow." Thinking ahead, she pointed and asked, "Can you bring it up with that tub of lights and clips?"

Chris looked even more disgruntled, but he was here to work. She wasn't paying him to stand around on his phone. He knew that. He was just in a mood. He groaned as he ascended the ladder, carrying the tub tucked under one arm and the tape measure gripped in his bare fist. Where were his gloves?

Holly reached down and took both items from him. Before he could go back down, she said, "Since you're up here, how about you help me with these lights. Do you remember the layout?"

Chris nodded and hoisted himself up onto the rooftop. Holly opened the tub and started attaching clips along the wires. She used her tape measure to lay out the grid lines. Chris started feeding her the wires of lights, adding clips as he went for her to attach to the shingles.

They worked in silence until Chris spoke. His voice was low, but in the crisp silence from the blanket of snow surrounding them she could hear him clearly. "I have a tournament this weekend."

Holly scrunched her lips together, thinking quickly, trying to remember if he'd joined a team or something. "Oh, yeah, that's cool. Did you join a sports team?"

Chris snorted. "Yeah right."

Holly stopped what she was doing and looked back at him. He was talking to her, so she needed to listen. "Okay, what's the tournament for?"

Chris didn't meet her eyes when he answered. "It's a gaming competition."

Oh, now that was definitely a sport he excelled at. "This weekend, huh?" Ahh. *Therein lies the rub.* This weekend was Christmas Eve and there were many Santa's Village activities scheduled all day on both days. "I know you didn't forget about the calendar events for Santa's Village, so I'm guessing you're choosing to bow out." Holly set the tape measure down and shifted her legs, turning so she was sitting on her butt to take some pressure off her knees.

Chris shrugged his broad shoulders beneath his black hoodie. "Yeah. I want to focus on the game I'm good at. Not always follow along with family obligations. I know Dad wants me to be more involved. With the elf stuff. And with the roofing business, but I...I just don't want to," his voice trailed off. Holly figured he was likely saying these feelings out loud for the first time and she was proud of him.

"Being the youngest, I know you feel a lot of pressure."

"You do too, Holly. As the oldest you think you have to be a part of everything—" Chris cut off his words, maybe thinking he'd overstepped. But he was right. She'd just accepted she had that problem last night.

Holly nodded and reached for his leg. She patted his jeans before sitting back up and sighing. "I do. And I'm tired of it too, buddy. You're not alone in that. I just came to that realization last night. It'll take some time to extract myself from some things, but it won't happen overnight. I think this'll be my last year as an elf. It's time to hang up my pointy shoes."

Chris laughed. "I'm glad. I want to also. It's gotten to be really embarrassing for me. I just don't want to do it anymore. And I don't want to take over the family business," he blurted, his words rushing together. He took a couple deep breaths before continuing. "I want to go to college for gaming and coding. I want to develop new games, not be a roofer."

These were likely the most words he'd spoken to her in quite some time. She was glad he felt comfortable sharing his feelings with her. "Well, one thing is, the company name is Noelle Roofing, not Noelle and Son Roofing. So you shouldn't feel any obligation to carry on the business. Dad's not expecting you to. Have you talked to him about this?"

Chris shook his head and dropped his gaze to his fingernails.

"Plus, you might want to talk to Eve about that anyway. I think she has plans to take over the business when Dad's ready to pass the reins. I'm happy in the background, sitting at my desk, plugging in numbers."

"Nerd," he scoffed.

"You're just jealous," she fired back with a laugh. Once her laughter tapered off, she knew she needed to end this while he was still engaged. "Talk to Mom and Dad. They'll understand about this weekend. We have plenty of people signed up to help with the Santa meet-and-greet."

Chris looked up at her, his eyes solemn but hopeful. "You think so?"

For his sake, she hoped so.

Chapter Four

Gabe glanced at his watch. His grandpa was supposed to meet him at eleven. It was five till and he'd already readied the plane. He'd moved it out of the hangar about thirty minutes ago. The pre-flight check was complete and all he was waiting on was his passenger.

A dark blue Chevy Camaro roared onto the tarmac. His grandpa was behind the wheel. Working at the Chevrolet Plant he got a new car every couple of years. This was the one he'd chosen when he retired. Seeing an eighty-year-old at the wheel was something else. He hoped he looked as cool as Joseph Shepherd when he was his age.

Gabe leaned back against the plane with his arms crossed over his chest. After his run this morning he showered and changed into more appropriate attire for this weather. He wore worn jeans, boots, a sweater and a leather jacket. Aviator glasses knocked down the glare of the bright sky reflected off the patches of snow around the tarmac. The snow had stopped falling about an hour ago.

"Howdy, Gabriel!" Joseph called out as he exited his sports car.

Gabe shook his head at the picture, then pushed off the plane. He greeted him with a handshake when he approached, as he'd been doing since the day they first met. But his grandpa always pulled him in for a hug. Gabe just wasn't comfortable initiating contact like that yet. But it did warm his heart to be welcomed like this.

He hadn't known what to expect when he'd first met the man who fathered his mother. He didn't know if he'd be a big man or a small man, be bald or have a head full of hair, be mean and gruff, or kind and curious.

Joseph Shepherd was shorter than Gabe, but that could just be from age. Or he'd gotten his height from the other half of his genes. The man had a head full of white hair and a quick smile. Gabe saw his square jaw and green eyes shining back at him.

And Joseph was the kindest man he'd ever met.

But he still wasn't comfortable calling him grandpa to his face. He'd settled on Joseph for now.

"So, you really know how to fly this thing."

"Yes, sir. Just think about the movie Top Gun. That was the training I received. I've been flying planes much more powerful than this one for more than a decade," Gabe reassured him. "Plane's ready, so let's hop on board." Gabe guided him over to the passenger side and opened the door for him. His grandpa was pretty nimble for his age, but he stood nearby just in case the old man needed assistance climbing in.

After securely shutting the door, Gabe circled the plane once before climbing in his side. Once he was settled inside, he handed Joseph a set of headphones. "It gets really loud once I flip the engine on. We'll be able to communicate through these."

Joseph sat back in his seat and placed the headphones on his ears. Gabe watched as he clicked his seatbelt together. Then Gabe did the same. For this being his first time in a plane he wasn't showing any nerves, outwardly at least.

Gabe went through the start-up procedures, talking his grandpa through each of the steps. Starting with the parking brake, circuit breakers, and avionics master switch. Next, he pointed out the fuel and throttle settings. Gabe warned his grandpa about the next step so he wouldn't be alarmed before he opened his window and shouted outside, "Clear prop!"

Gabe turned the key, and the engine roared to life. Looking over, he gave Joseph the thumbs up. The propellor spun so fast it was only a blur of color past the nose of the plane. He spoke to the control tower and got cleared to taxi.

"Ready?" Gabe looked over and found his grandpa smiling, looking eager for this new adventure. Joseph nodded and Gabe lined them up on their runway. The ground and trees became a blur as they hurtled down the runway, lifting off into the air once he reached the correct speed. The plane gracefully took flight, pleasing Gabe. This was one of the three planes that he would be acquiring upon completing the takeover.

"Have you had your meeting yet?" his grandpa called out through the microphone attached to the headphones reading Gabe's mind.

Gabe shook his head then glanced over briefly. "Not yet. It's in two days. I met with my lawyer yesterday."

"You think Amos is ready to sell?" Joseph's focus shifted from him back out to the scenery on his side of the plane. The rolling hills around them were covered in a white blanket.

Gabe nodded and kept his eyes trained outside the windshield. "I think so. He said he'd been hoping to retire for about two years now but hadn't found anyone interested in taking over his clients."

"You're the right man for the job."

Throughout his career he'd had a lot of encouragement and praise from his superiors, but this felt different. This spoke more to his heart than to his pride. It was hard not to think back and wish he'd had this man in his life when he was growing up. Gabe knew he would be a totally different person today if he'd had a stable upbringing. If he'd had that sense of belonging and acceptance that having a family gives a person.

"Amos Tucker's been ready to retire for longer than that. But he's been looking to hand his business over to someone younger." Joseph took his focus off the view outside his window to send a smile Gabe's way. "And that's you, son."

Enter Gabe, a retired Marine looking for something to do with the second half of his life. He'd been trained by the best and had the qualifications for the job.

He'd been mulling the idea around for the last couple months. His grandpa had actually been the one to suggest it once Joseph knew what Gabe's specialties had been while he was in the Marines. Joseph introduced them then let Gabe handle it from there.

The deal will be finalized this week. Amos already had the hangar space, the planes, the business name. All Gabe had to do was buy him out and take over the day-to-day lessons and training schedule. It was a massive undertaking, but Gabe was used to working and couldn't imagine truly being retired with nothing to do each day at age thirty-eight.

It was unthinkable.

It's not like he planned to spend his days at the country club or run a hot dog cart. He needed a full-time job that left him satisfied. He loved flying and he was a great teacher. Plus, he didn't actually have to work every day, just when he had a lesson scheduled. He could pick and choose. It was a win-win.

"Ryan's coming to visit soon," Gabe announced, keeping his eyes trained on the sky around them.

"I can't wait to meet him."

And Gabe knew he meant those words. It surprised him how quickly Joseph Shepherd had accepted Gabe into his life. Joseph knew a little about his time in service. And he'd heard about the guys, mostly Ryan, and said he'd hoped to get to meet them.

"Actually, I don't know when he's showing up. It could be today or next week. You never know with that guy." Gabe tried to bite off the grin that wanted to surface. "Oh, guess what his punk-ass did?"

Joseph looked over, his eyes focused on him. He looked ready to hear something good. Gabe knew he wouldn't disappoint with this story.

"You know that Christmas time isn't my favorite. All the decorations and events seem a little over the top to me," he said with a shrug. His grandpa didn't know all the details about what it was like growing up with his mom, only what he'd hand-picked to share. Joseph just knew that they'd struggled. His grandpa could deduce that there hadn't been much money for presents and all the trimmings. "The guys know that and decided as their retirement present to me to have *Deck This House* come out and do just that."

Joseph started laughing and only continued when Gabe described in detail what he'd come home to.

"That's priceless," he finally said when he could catch his breath. "That's what you call getting punked, isn't it? My boy, that shows that they really care about you. Not because they thought you would hate it and get mad at them, but it shows that they know you and learned about you over the years."

Gabe's lips twitched. "It is pretty funny actually. But I was mad at first. I called the company right away and asked them to come take everything down."

"No!" Sharp green eyes similar to his own turned his way. "That poor girl. She works so hard."

"She said they have a strict policy to keep the decorations up for at least three weeks before they come take them down. Do you know her?" Gabe asked looking over to see his grandpa's expression.

"Yes. I know her family. They've lived here in Tinsel for generations. I worked with her grandfather at the Chevrolet Plant. We both retired about the same time. Her parents run a roofing business and are the key players in Santa's Village in the park. Her dad is Santa and his kids dress up as elves to help with the children getting pictures with Santa."

Holly dresses up as an elf?

That was something he had to see. Immediately, his mind flashed to a sexy, naughty-list elf costume complete with sheer hose, spiked heels, short skirt, and a tight tank showing lots of cleavage.

But he was probably wrong since it was for kids. Disappointment flooded through him at the thought.

***

Squeals of joy greeted Holly when she got out of her truck. The colorful lights adorning every surface of the park grabbed her attention first. The ice-skating rink had just opened this morning, and she knew the kids couldn't be happier. She saw many adults out there as well.

Ice-skating had never been her thing. She just didn't have the balance for it. Even though she was nimble on a roof and a ladder and felt like she had good balance for that, putting herself on narrow blades and moving over uneven ice wasn't her favorite thing to do.

Her sister Eve was a natural. Even Chris was really good.

Holly set her elf hat on her head, adjusting it in the side mirror of her truck before joining the crowd of people milling about. Couples were holding hands. Kids skirted in and around adults moving at a slower pace. *Jingle Bells* played from the speakers hung on light poles. The snow on the ground added to the scene before her and made it a perfect winter wonderland.

Live reindeer were in a paddock being fed hay from excited children. She waved at Debbie and Mike, the handlers who brought them to town every holiday season. Next up on her path was a new event this year, a Christmas Tree maze. Glowing bulbs were strung in a cris-cross pattern over the tops of the lined-up trees. She heard people calling out from inside the maze, followed by laughter. She'll have to try it out soon.

Holly arrived at the row of food trucks. She couldn't help but pause at the one selling hot chocolate. Since the line wasn't too long, she zipped over and got behind her first-grade teacher. After greeting her, Holly's gaze bounced around the area, recognizing many faces in the crowd.

The park was bustling. So much joy and happiness oozed out of the space that her mood instantly improved. She really did love this time of year. The itch to move on from this responsibility was spreading though and she'd have to address it soon.

Seriously, she'd been dressing in an elf costume for the month of December each year since she was twelve years old.

When Chris had mentioned being embarrassed today, she could totally relate.

Her gaze caught on a man who looked a lot like her unhappy client, Gabriel Shepherd, walking near the ice-skating rink, but she immediately dismissed it. There was no way he'd be here.

Her mind flashed to him standing before her this morning in running shorts. What had the man been thinking? Snow had been falling. His legs were hot though, hitting well over a ten on the sexy meter. She had no idea how he could go out like that. She would have turned into a popsicle before she'd even left the driveway.

Once Holly's order was ready, she sipped her hot chocolate to warm herself up. Her thoughts and the cold breeze blowing through her fleece leggings caused a chill to skate down her spine.

Or could that chill be more of a tingle because she thought the man in question was sexy?

Maybe a little bit of both. Holly hid her grin behind the lip of the cup.

Passing between the six-foot-tall Nutcrackers she entered the Santa meet-and-greet zone. Eve stood near the photo area. Her sister looked a little frazzled, with her hands twisted in knots. Her eyes seemed to be scanning the crowd. Kids were already trickling in. Santa wouldn't be out in his chair for another twenty minutes, but people were anxious with only five days left before Christmas.

The line was long, but no one showed any signs of getting unruly.

Yet. It was still early.

Holly immediately got pulled into the fray when Eve spotted her. "Holly!"

Waving, she took another sip of her beloved hot chocolate before setting it down on the table positioned beside her mom's camera set-up. "Hi! What is it? You look upset."

Eve grabbed Holly's elbows and whisper-shouted, "The photo printer isn't working!"

Holly took a deep breath, bringing her focus to the problem at hand. Twenty minutes until opening and the printer that prints out the photos of Santa with the children waiting in line wasn't working. Definitely a problem.

Okay, no need to panic. They'd just get another one.

"Where's Mom? Does Dad know?"

"She's calling the shop in town. Dad doesn't know." Eve's hazel eyes were wide, and she was starting to shiver. Holly rubbed her hands up and down Eve's arms.

"Have you looked at it yet?" Holly asked, stepping around her sister to the printer sitting before the camera tripod. The power was on but there was an error message written in the display window.

"I don't know anything about printers!" she cried out.

Holly looked back over her shoulder at her sister. Quirking her eyebrow at her caused Eve to take in a deep breath. "Sorry. You're right. No need to panic. It's just five days before Christmas and there's a line around the park waiting to meet with Santa and share their Christmas wishes—"

Eve stopped talking when a man about their age crossed the red velvet rope and spoke to them. "Hi. I'm sorry, I couldn't help but over-hear."

Holly gave her sister another quirked-eye-brow look, then turned toward the man. He was in a suit and tie and held the hand of a little girl in a velvety red dress with green ribbons in her blonde hair.

"Yes, we're having a little malfunction," Holly explained.

"I work with computers and printers all the time. Would you like me to look at it for you?" His blue eyes bounced between the two of them. The sisters both released a sigh at his offer.

"Yes, please." Holly stepped back and waved her hand in the direction of the printer. "Thank you so much for volunteering. I hope it's an easy fix."

The little girl followed closely behind the man, presumably her father. Her eyes were the same shade of blue. When he squatted down in front of the printer, he squeezed her hand before releasing it. She huddled close to his back, obviously shy. Eve reached into the basket they had on the table and asked him first if she could offer his daughter a peppermint.

He looked back up at her and smiled, nodding. "Thank you."

"No, thank you," Eve said then knelt down to speak to the little girl.

Holly kept one eye on them and the other on the man currently bent over their printer. She watched as he popped the backing off and started shifting metal parts around. He pulled out his phone and brought up a search engine. Tapping in the error code he quickly scanned a video about how to fix it.

Ten minutes later, he popped the cover back in place and hit the power button. To their relief the error message was gone. "Now, do a test print to make sure it's running right."

Eve popped her mom's camera off its stand and turned to the man and his daughter. "Care to pose for one?"

"Sure." The man picked his daughter up in his arm and tickled her chin, bringing a smile to her extra-red peppermint lips. Eve snapped the shot then sent the photo to the printer. They all stood watching, Holly's insides knotting up the longer it took to process. Then the printer lurched to life and creaked and groaned out a color photo of the father and daughter who had come to their rescue.

"Christmas is saved!" Eve cried out. She took the photo and put it in a frame and slipped it in a bag before handing it to the man. "This one is on the house. Thank you so much for your assistance."

The man accepted the shopping bag and smiled. Holly noticed how her sister seemed to melt from the heat of it.

"I'm Matt," the man said, shifting the gift bag to the hand holding the little girl, reaching out to shake hers. "And this is my daughter, Annabelle."

Eve shook his hand, her smile all but glowing. "It's a pleasure to meet you, Matt. And Annabelle," Eve added slipping her another peppermint stick. "I'm Eve and this is my sister Holly."

Matt nodded to Holly, but his smile appeared to be only for Eve. Interesting. No ring on his left hand. She'd have to make sure Eve was aware.

"Would you like to move to the front of the line as a thank you?" Eve asked.

Matt shook his head. "No, we couldn't do that. We'll wait in the line where we were. But thank you for the offer."

"Well, then, Merry Christmas, Annabelle! Merry Christmas, Matt." Eve waved and watched them retreat back under the red rope and resume their place in line.

How's that for getting the heart rate up before her shift even started? Who was she kidding, thinking about her grumpy grinch in his sexy running shorts had already made that happen.

Chapter Five

Gabe spent the afternoon with his grandpa before heading to the grocery on his way home. He'd need to stock up with Ryan coming.

Ryan was about his age, an inch taller, and had about twenty more pounds of muscle on him than Gabe. Built like a tank, he ate like his life depended on it. The man needed constant fuel.

Gabe stocked up on meat and vegetables. He even tossed some of those oven lasagnas in his cart. He was looking forward to having company. Ryan will be his first guest. Last night after he'd gotten off the phone, he'd gone straight to the guest room and started moving furniture so that it functioned as one, instead of the discard pile it had been. He broke down the boxes and stored clothes and linens in the appropriate closets. He'd made the bed and then vacuumed the cleaned-up space. He was ready for whenever Ryan showed up.

The sky was dark when he left the grocery. He heard a bell ringing and dug the change he'd received from the cashier out of his pocket and placed it in the red bucket. The man thanked him and Gabe nodded his head. "Have a good night."

He might not like the holiday season but he liked to help where he could, especially after having been on the receiving end of the Salvation Army a time or two when he was growing up.

Gabe loaded his bags in the back seat of the truck then returned his cart to the store so the workers wouldn't have to come retrieve it. The second he cranked the engine he heard "Let It Snow" on the radio and pushed the button off. He might be able to avert his eyes to all the decorations, but he didn't want any of that cheer inside the cab with him.

He was thinking about what he was going to make for dinner when he absentmindedly turned into his driveway. It took his brain a moment to catch up to his eyes. It was like déjà vu.

All the lights were aglow and the blowups were full and bobbing in the breeze. The reindeer he'd spotted from the porch last night were actually animatronic, their heads rising and lowering.

"What the hell?"

Gabe put the truck in park and realized belatedly that there was a car in his driveway. A furrow appeared between his brows as he grabbed his keys and stepped out. He was greeted immediately by a familiar voice.

"What the fuck were you complaining about? This is awesome!"

Ryan.

That asshole.

Ryan Blaylock leaned over the railing of his porch, arms up and wide open, his smile just as wide to match. "This is beautiful. I think Frosty is my favorite."

Gabe shook his head and tried not to roll his eyes. He headed back to the truck to unload the groceries. "Come make yourself useful."

Ryan loped down the porch steps and followed him back to the driver's side. He took the bags that Gabe held out to him. "Good to see you too, buddy."

Gabe looked over at his grinning face. He too sported a high and tight, but his blond hair was light enough he almost looked bald. It was good to see him. This was the longest time they'd been apart since meeting over a decade ago.

Ryan was family to him, and he'd missed his arrogant ass.

"You too, Ry."

Gabe reached out and Ryan slammed his chest into Gabe's. They both engaged in a manly, back-slapping hug before taking the bags up to the house.

"How long have you been here?"

Ryan glanced at his watch. "About two hours."

Gabe looked at him, eyes wide. "Dude! Why didn't you call me?"

"I figured you were busy," Ryan said with a shrug.

"I was hanging out with Joseph—with my grandpa." Gabe kicked the door closed behind them and led the way to the kitchen.

"See, busy." Ryan nodded. "Doing something important and I didn't want to interrupt." He added his bags to the island then started unloading them. They worked together to get all the groceries put away. "Have you had dinner yet?"

"No, I was thinking of making this lasagna."

Ryan shook his head, his brown eyes bright. "Nah, let's go out. It's on me. Show me your new town, Gabe. I want the whole experience."

Gabe thought that was the worst idea. He had no desire to tour Ryan around Tinsel in the heart of the Christmas season. He just wanted to eat something hearty and sit on his couch the rest of the night.

"I can see your gears turning, trying to think of a way out of this, but there's no way, no how, Sarg." Ryan slapped his palms together and rubbed them. "I'm ready to see it all. I saw some of it on my drive through town from Nashville. I saw food trucks and a whole lot going on in a park downtown."

Great. Santa's Village. Just what he wanted. His worst nightmare.

Ryan grabbed Gabe's keys off the island and held them out.

Guess his chance for a peaceful evening on the couch watching football was out. Gabe grumbled incoherently and snatched the keys from his buddy's hand. "Come on," he growled.

"That's the spirit." Ryan laughed and grabbed Gabe's shoulders when he passed, gripping them tight. "You got this, Sarg. Living here now, you gotta get passed it somehow."

Yeah, somehow.

Immersion therapy.

On the drive back downtown Ryan kept up his side of the chatter, filling Gabe in on all that the platoon had been doing since he'd retired. Gabe definitely missed parts of it, but doing recon exercises or training after sleepless nights, not so much. He'd loved it when he was in his twenties, but being in his late thirties, his body didn't appreciate that kind of treatment anymore.

"Man, they go all out," Ryan exclaimed when they turned down Main Street. The park was off to the west and there were cars everywhere. He had no idea where they'd find parking with this crowd. "There's one!" Ryan said, pointing to the right.

A minivan was backing out of a space on a side road. Gabe signaled and parked in the space when they left. Throwing the truck in park, he let out a deep sigh. Resigned.

"There ya go, that's the spirit. Acceptance." Ryan slapped his shoulder then exited his side of the truck. Gabe reluctantly followed.

He felt bombarded immediately after opening the driver's door. "Santa's Coming To Town" blasted from speakers overhead. Squeals of delight could be heard as they walked by the ice-skating rink. Ryan headed off toward the row of food trucks, letting his stomach lead the way. Gabe tucked his hands in the pockets of his leather jacket and wished he'd grabbed his beanie before heading out the door.

Savory smells reached him and Gabe perked up. He liked food. What did he care if he had to eat it while Dean Martin crooned about it beginning to look a lot like Christmas? And, yes, he could recognize the Rat Pack. Even if one of them was singing a Christmas Carol. He'd loved listening to that kind of music when he'd been a kid. One of the houses he'd stayed in had a record player. The dad had a serious collection and liked sharing with Gabe about who he'd called the "oldies but goodies." That had been his favorite house. He'd only been there about five months before the holidays had rolled around and money was too tight to keep him there any longer. That had been the second saddest moment in his life. His mother's death being the first.

Gabe shook off the memory when he realized Ryan was calling his name. Ryan had stopped in the road, and the crowd flowed around him like he was an ice breaker. *Get your shit together, Gabe.* Doing another mental shake to remove the images his mind had just resurrected, he locked it in and focused on Ryan and the search for food.

"Which one sounds good? Mexican, fair food or hot chocolate?"

"Hot chocolate is not a food." Gabe looked around at the trucks and read their menu boards set up outside. "I could go for a steak taco."

"Nothing says Christmas like Mexican food," Ryan drawled pushing Gabe in the right direction. Gabe chuckled and put in his order. Ryan ordered twice as much and they stepped to the side to wait for their food.

Gabe's eyes were drawn to the gazebo with its garland and lights. The big guy in red sat on a gold-colored throne with three kids crowded around him. He could practically see the man's eyes twinkling from here. The scene looked like any Christmas movie ever made.

"This place is hopping. We never had anything like this where I grew up."

"That's because you grew up in Miami," he quipped. "Not much of a winter wonderland there."

Ryan shrugged and kept looking around. Gabe's gaze followed and happened to catch on one of the elves on the stage near the big guy. Her dark brown hair hung loose under her red and green elf hat. Her blue eyes were definitely twinkling. As were her dimples.

Gabe's heart started pounding in his chest. He had no idea why he'd react to the woman from *Deck This House* this way. His grandpa said she dressed up as an elf during Christmastime. Of course, he'd pictured her outfit to be a little more risqué than what she was currently wearing, but the skirt and blouse looked good on her.

"What's caught your attention?" Ryan asked, shifting to stand next to him. "You wanna go see Santa?"

"Fuck off, Ry," he grumbled. Ryan only laughed in response, not offended by his tone at all.

"Is it one of the elves? The one holding the hand of those two little girls, she's hot—"

"Shut it."

Ryan turned his intent gaze on Gabe. "Oh, is she someone you know? Are you already interested in her? Have you been holding out on me?" His voice got louder with each question.

"Quit it with the questions." Gabe turned to face the food truck, putting his back to the gazebo and the woman who'd most certainly caught his eye. "I don't know her at all. She's the woman from *Deck This House*."

"No way! That babe is the one who put up all those awesome decorations? I have to go thank her," Ryan said stepping away. Gabe reached out and grabbed his arm, pulling him back. The instant he saw Ryan's grin Gabe knew he'd been played.

"Asshole," he mumbled and headed for the order window when he heard their number shouted out.

"Seriously, I will have to thank her. She did a great job. The town has decorations up every-where. I wonder if she did them all." Ryan grabbed his plate with a thank you to the cook. They found a spot at a table lit up by strings of lights overhead.

Now Gabe was wondering the same. If so, she'd been helluva busy and certainly didn't have time to come take his decorations down. She probably hadn't even had time to stop by his house this morning to check on his grumpy ass. He needed to apologize again.

Gabe dug into his steak tacos instead. It wasn't like he could do it now. She was busy doing what elves do, and he wouldn't disturb her. Maybe he could call her tomorrow or stop by her office. He had no idea if she even had an office.

"Finish up. Man, you eat so slow." Gabe looked down at the last half of his third taco then over at Ryan's empty plate. The man had eaten six tacos in the time he'd eaten two and a half. He wasn't slow; Ryan was too fast. Always had been. He couldn't believe the guy wasn't plagued with indigestion and heartburn all the time.

Gabe rolled his eyes and savored the last two bites of his meal. Mexican may not say Christ-mas but it was delicious. He glanced at the company name and decided he'd definitely eat their food again. Tossing his trash into the can near the tables he tucked his hands back into his pockets.

"I'm thirsty," Ryan announced. "Let's see if there's any beer."

Gabe didn't think there would be. It was a family event not a rock concert. But he followed his buddy, dodging children running all around. Just as they passed the hot chocolate truck another pack of kids sprinted towards him, a young boy wearing a Santa hat leading the race, and Gabe quickly sidestepped, turning his body ninety degrees to avoid a collision.

His back bumped into someone and he heard them release a loud "Oomph" upon impact. The first thing he saw when he turned around was a red and green elf hat and dark hair. Her back was turned and she was hunched over. He quickly moved around to see the front of her and couldn't help his loud intake of breath, sucked in through clenched teeth.

Holly stood frozen before him, hunched over, her arm aloft holding a half-empty paper cup of hot chocolate. The other half was currently dripping from her nose and chin.

Gabe felt a bunch of napkins plop onto his shoulder and reached up to grab them. *Thank you, Ryan.* "I'm so sorry," Gabe quickly said and started using the napkins to mop up the spill. He felt odd wiping her face, but she seemed fine with it. And maybe still a little stunned. He hoped the hot liquid hadn't burned her. "Are you okay? Did you get burned?"

Holly cleared her throat and held her hand out for the rest of the napkins. Gabe passed them over and took the cup from her hand. "Thank you," she mumbled. "Not for the soak, mind you," she clarified, "but for holding my cup. And the napkins."

He watched her wipe the rest of the residue from her chin and then lastly her nostrils.

"Thankfully, Ms. Tessie doesn't serve it too hot. She doesn't want to hurt the kids."

He stepped back over to the truck and asked for another cup. Ms. Tessie had seen the spill and already had one in hand to pass to him. "Thank you, Ms. Tessie," Gabe said.

Gabe returned to her side and held the new cup out to her. "Oh, thank you. You didn't have to do that. I probably needed to be cut off any-way," Holly added, wadding the napkins up in her hands, before accepting the fresh new cup from him. "You can enjoy that one if you'd like. It's backwash free. I hadn't even had my first sip yet."

Gabe looked down at the brown liquid. He couldn't remember if he'd ever had hot choco-late before.

"You've never had hot chocolate before?"

Gabe must have said that out loud. He cleared his throat then said, "Too sweet for me."

"The sweeter the better for me." Holly's dim-ples winked out with her smile. He could pic-ture that. She looked like she enjoyed all things sugary and sweet. Gabe reached up and tipped her hat to the right. He must have knocked it askew. "Thank you," she said reaching up to touch her hat, a sheepish grin on her face. Up close, he realized her blouse was more fitted than he'd imagined for a children's event.

It didn't put her on the naughty list, but it definitely brought her curves to his attention. She had to be freezing though.

"Drink up," he said. "You need to stay warm. You must be freezing."

"I am over here." She pointed with her cup. "There are heaters up on the gazebo so I can't layer up too much or I'd be dripping with sweat under all those lights."

Gabe's gaze remained on the gazebo and he watched Santa laugh loudly at something one of the children said. "So that's your dad, huh?"

Holly nodded. "Yep, he's been playing the part of the big guy since I was a little kid."

Ryan came to stand by Gabe's shoulder. "Hi, I'm Ryan Blaylock." Ryan extended his right hand toward Holly. "I wanted to personally thank you for what you did. The lights and all the decorations are beautiful and just what I wanted to surprise him with."

Holly chuckled as she accepted his hand-shake. "You surprised him all right." Gabe enjoyed how her face lit up when she laughed. He hoped it was over the topic and not because of the six-foot-four dude standing beside him. "I'm Holly. I'm not sure it was a pleasant surprise though," she added, side-eyeing Gabe.

"Oh, don't let his grumpy side fool you, he's a teddy bear underneath that prickly outer layer."

"Ryan," Gabe started but then he realized Ryan was still shaking her hand. "Enough."

Ryan immediately dropped her hand. "Holly, it was a pleasure meeting you. Keep up the good work. Both with the lights and your selfless elfish work."

Her eyes widened and she looked like she was about to bolt. "Oh, speaking of. My break is definitely over. I need to get back," she said looking over her shoulder toward the gazebo.

Ryan, thankfully, took his cue and left the conversation, backing up behind him somewhere. Gabe wanted to keep talking to her. The sound of her voice, sweet and soothing, made his heart pound extra hard. The twin divots in her cheeks were mesmerizing, and he could get lost in them for days. Searching for something to keep her interested he blurted out, "Have you ever been flying?"

Holly tilted her head and her left eyebrow quirked up to meet the edge of her elf hat. The lights hanging above them reflecting in her eyes.

"In a small plane," he quickly added. "Not just on a commercial aircraft."

Holly shook her head. Gabe watched her silky hair slide across her shoulders. "No, I haven't. Only on a big plane and just once when I went to Seattle with my college friends."

Silence followed. He'd gotten caught up in her gorgeous blue gaze.

"Why do you ask?"

Her voice snapped him out of his trance. "I'd like to take you up."

Holly's hand holding her hot chocolate paused mid-way to her mouth and her eyes jerked to his. "Up where?"

Gabe grinned and pointed up. "Up there."

Holly's eyebrows furrowed. "You want to take me up there? In a plane?"

"That's the easiest way."

She gave him a quizzical look. "You're a pilot?"

"It would be hard to do otherwise," he stated matter-of-factly, but hoped it came off as light sarcasm. "I'm a retired Marine with over ten years' experience in planes."

"He can fly anything!"

Gabe's head tilted back as he straightened. *That jackass. I'd thought he'd left us alone.* His eyes drifted closed and he couldn't help the head shake that followed.

Holly chuckled then sipped her hot chocolate, glancing over his shoulder, presumably at Ryan. "Wow. Anything?"

"Yep!" Ryan called out, then his voice quieted as he approached. "He even flew a helicopter once but that was behind enemy—"

"Ry!" Gabe cut him off, turning to add a glare.

"What? It was impressive, dude. And that other time," he slapped the back of his hand against Gabe's shoulder, "I had to patch you up when you flew us—" Gabe's growl cut him off. "What? No?"

Gabe glanced back and saw Holly's shocked expression. "Sorry, he's an ass."

Wide blue eyes met his. Snapping her jaw closed, she asked, "Wait? Patch you up? Were you injured?"

"He talks too much," he grumbled and shoved Ryan away. Then Gabe smiled, hoping to distract her from that topic. "Back to my invitation. Would you like to go up?" Then inspiration struck. "I think you'd enjoy seeing all the Christmas lights from above."

"Oh," she sighed, her mouth lifting into a grin, "that sounds amazing. Thank you. Yes, I think I'd like that. Only because you sold me with the lights idea," she added with a wink. "I'm going to be nervous as hell. Just warning you."

Gabe shook his head once. "No, you won't. You're going to be so distracted up there that you won't have time to be nervous," he said confidently. "When's your next free night?"

Holly pursed her lips and looked up. "Let me think, hmm." Her gaze bounced back to his and she grinned. "Tomorrow."

"Tomorrow," he repeated, his lips curving to match hers. "Can I pick you up or would you like to meet me at the airport?"

"I'll send you my address." Holly raised her eyebrows at him and laughed. "That's going to be a first for me."

Ryan started clearing his throat. Repeatedly. And loudly. Gabe wanted to ignore him, but the dude wouldn't stop. Finally, Gabe jerked a look at him over his shoulder and saw Ryan gesturing upward with his chin. Gabe frowned and shook his head at him, wishing he could shoo him away like a pesky fly.

Holly chuckled, bringing his attention back to her. He quickly dropped his scowl. She pointed above them, then gave him a sheepish grin. Gabe looked up but he didn't see anything. Glancing back at Holly he was about to ask her what they were looking at when she grabbed his leather jacket in her fist and pulled him towards her.

Gabe, totally caught off guard and off balance, was stunned when her lips softly touched his. The impact nearly stopped his heart and short-circuited his brain. But his nerves were on overload. And what he was feeling was heat. Desire. Electricity pulsing through his veins.

Before he could get his brain to engage his arms to reach out and touch her, wanting to draw her closer, she pulled back, her hand relaxing, then smoothing over the crumpled leather.

Their gazes met, her eyes shifting between his and his mouth. Her tongue darted out to lick her lower lip and he nearly whimpered.

He wanted another taste.

He wanted to deepen that kiss.

He wanted to consume her.

"See you tomorrow," she whispered, then backed away. She waved at them both before turning for the gazebo.

Gabe tucked the hand not holding the cup of now-cold chocolate into his pocket to keep from reaching for her, hauling her back to him for another kiss. He was blown away. The kiss had been on the sweet side, but the heat had been off the charts.

"You're welcome."

Ryan.

But this time he did deserve thanks. Gabe hadn't recognized the mistletoe hanging above him. "Thanks, Ry."

Ryan gripped his shoulder with one hand and slapped him on the chest with the other and asked, "So, inquiring minds want to know...are you already a member of the mile-high club?"

Chapter Six

Holly set the hair dryer down on the counter and pulled a comb through her straight locks. As a kid she'd hated having straight hair, always envious of friends with waves or curls. She'd begged her mom to get a perm when she was in middle school. That had been a disaster.

Now, as an adult she cherished her healthy, silky hair. It took a lot to put curl in it, so she didn't do it often. After glancing at her phone, she decided she didn't have enough time to do it tonight. She'd have to settle for keeping it straight, figuring it would be under her hat most of the time anyway.

Gabe said he'd pick her up at a quarter to five. She'd tried to leave work early, but her dad had called her in for a meeting about a new contract they'd gotten, throwing off her plan to be ready early. She'd jumped in the shower as soon as she'd made it home and had about fifteen minutes to spare right now.

Swiping on some eyeliner and a cranberry-flavored lip gloss, she called things done.

She hoped he liked the taste of cranberries. That kiss they'd shared last night had stayed with her throughout sleep, creating some very sexy dreams.

Satisfied with how she looked, her lips curved up so that her dimples showed. That was another feature she had gotten from her mom. This trait she shared with all her siblings.

The doorbell rang.

"Wow, he's early," she whispered, dashing from the bathroom to pull on her coat and grab her gear. She had no idea how cold it would be up there so she had a bag packed with her hat, scarf and gloves. She tossed her purse in the bag too and pulled open the door, tugging the straps over her shoulder.

"Hi," she greeted, her smile blooming when she saw the picture he made standing on her front stoop in more appropriate attire for the season. Well-worn jeans, boots and a green sweater peeked out of the top of his black jacket, looking like an Eddie Bauer ad.

Gabe's smile was as bright as the golden lights glowing all around her doorway. "Hi. Ready?" he asked.

Pulling her door closed, she nodded. "It's a nice night for flying, right?" she asked glancing up at the sky, still a bright pink from the sinking sun. The clouds had cleared out today. No more snow in the forecast until Christmas Eve.

"It's perfect." His grin reassured her. "The half-moon tonight will provide enough light but it won't be so bright that you can't see the lights." Gabe stepped back and let her lead the way down the walk to her driveway. At his truck, he opened the passenger door for her and waited for her to get seated before closing it.

Holly noticed that his truck was very tidy. Working out of her truck made it hard to keep hers this clean. It even smelled like a new vehicle.

After climbing in, Gabe turned the key, adjusting the heating vents. "Are you cold?"

"No, this is perfect."

"I hope this wasn't too early for you." Gabe backed out of her drive and headed towards the airport. "Since it's the winter solstice and the shortest amount of daylight, I wanted you to be up there to see the transition time from sunset to dark skies."

"That sounds amazing. Actually, it worked out perfectly," she assured him. "I had one decorating job this morning, then spent the rest of the day at the roofing office working on invoices."

Gabe stopped at a red light and glanced her way, his green eyes focusing on hers. "That sounds like a busy day."

Holly nodded. "I keep busy. This time of year is pretty hectic with *Deck This House*, the roofing business and Santa's Village. But it isn't always like that."

"What do you do at the roofing business?" Gabe drove along the highway, glancing over at her periodically. Holly shifted in her seat towards him, taking this opportunity to check him out. His profile appeared chiseled from stone. A prominent brow sat above his gorgeous eyes. A straight nose pointed to a pair of masculine lips she couldn't wait to kiss again. Smooth skin covered a square jaw making her wonder if he just recently shaved. Strong hands wrapped around the steering wheel, and he appeared to be a very competent driver. She hoped that carried over to flying as well.

"My parents own Noelle Roofing. I work in the accounting office, keeping track of all the invoices for jobs and supplies."

"Sounds like they have a thriving business. How young were you the first time you got on a roof?" The dash lights highlighted the grin he flashed her way.

Holly laughed. "I probably climbed to the top of a ladder when I was three, but actually up on the roof with a tool, that was more likely closer to six. I started out doing the grunt work of scraping shingles when I was a teenager. But luckily, I figured out I really enjoyed numbers and making spreadsheets."

"Thankfully, there are people like you in the world."

Holly grinned. "Not a numbers guy, huh?"

He shook his head. "I can hold my own. Flying involves lots of math, but I'm definitely not a spreadsheet guy." He definitely sneered at the word *spreadsheet*. Which made her laugh because spreadsheets were her jam.

Gabe pulled into the airport and parked in an empty spot. "I already brought the plane out, but I'll need to do another pre-flight check since I left her unattended. I had a guy named Dave watching her, but I don't leave anything to chance." *Good to know.*

All of this was so foreign to her. She'd never been to a small airport like this or seen a plane up close before. She was starting to feel butterflies dancing in her belly again. She'd felt them for the first time last night, the instant her lips had touched his.

She couldn't believe how bold she'd been.

His friend Ryan had tried to get Gabe to look up with all his throat-clearing shenanigans. She'd noticed the mistletoe, but she didn't think Gabe recognized it. In that moment, she'd had a wild hair and decided to go for it. When their lips met, the butterflies danced, her heart thumped and heat coursed through her blood.

It was a simple kiss, but it had sizzled.

Holly hopped out when he opened her door for her. She accepted his hand to assist. His skin was so warm, and she felt a wee bit envious. She always felt cold. Deciding she'd like to share some of his warmth, she chose to walk closer to him than she probably should after knowing the man—with their first "meeting" being via phone—for not quite forty-eight hours.

Gabe moved closer, draping his arm around her waist. The heat coming off him felt amazing.

"Here she is," Gabe announced stopping when they were about twenty yards from a plane. Holly gulped. It was smaller than she'd imagined, again, having only been on a large commercial airliner. She found herself in that moment questioning her life choices. Was this thing safe? Gabe's hand tightened on her waist. "I get that seeing a plane this small might stir up some nerves, but I promise it's safe. The plane and me. I've been flying since I was in my twenties."

Holly gulped again. She had to get her nerves under control. "This is just a new experience, that's all. I've never even thought about flying in a plane this size, so I just need a few moments to get used to it." She reassured him with a grin and one succinct head nod.

Gabe dropped his arm, and she felt that loss of heat immediately.

"You'll get those few moments to adjust while I do my inspection. I'll call you over when I'm done, okay?" His arm slid down hers and he squeezed her fingers briefly before stepping away.

Holly nodded, enjoying all his touches. Something else that brought her joy—watching him walk away, his snug jeans outlining his firm ass to perfection. His walk was confident, and she could easily picture him in uniform striding towards his plane ready for a training mission. Last night she'd Googled images of Marine pilots so she could see what uniform they wore.

They'd looked similar to the images in her head of Maverick and Goose.

She could only imagine what he'd seen and done over his long career. Ryan had given her only a hint of what that might be when he'd overshared.

She watched intently while Gabe removed a clipboard from a compartment in the plane. He began marking things on the board as he moved around the plane. The sun was beginning to set, turning the sky many shades of pink and orange. Holly rubbed her hands together then reached into her bag to get her gloves. Putting them on she glanced up at the cloudless sky. She couldn't believe that she was about to be flying up there. Those butterflies began their ballet dance once again. Taking a couple deep breaths helped calm her racing heart. Just a smidge. She wasn't sure she'd be able to lose herself in the lights and not have time to be nervous like he'd predicted. But she was willing to try.

This would definitely go down in the books as the best first date ever.

Holly stomped her feet against the tarmac, trying to do it quietly. She didn't want to draw attention, but she needed to get her feet moving since the temp was dropping without the sun. It was likely in the mid-30s now and her feet were cold. She'd opted for pretty over practical tonight, and she was paying for it. She didn't have room in these boots for a pair of thick wool socks.

Finally, Gabe appeared to be wrapping it up. He waved her over and she took off towards him. As she approached, she pulled her phone from her jacket pocket because she had to snap at least one pic of this event. She caught him grinning at her, standing tall, hands in his pockets, the pink skies silhouetting the plane.

"Ready?" Gabe asked when she got close.

Holly tilted her head and answered honestly, "Yes, I am."

"That's the spirit." Gabe's wink set her heart rate to triple time. His smile so confident, while borderline cocky. She liked it. She liked it even more when he leaned toward her, his eyes searching hers, maybe waiting to see if she was willing. So instead of waiting, she met him halfway, pressing her lips to his. Hers felt cold against all his heat.

Warmth spread over her immediately, rushing through her veins, zinging all her nerves along the way.

Gabe pulled back, brushing his thumb across her tender lips. "Just wanted to give you something to occupy your mind with during take-off."

"Thank you for that," she said, her voice husky from the moment. She might just have to ask him for another if things started to get rocky. The rush of emotions she'd just experienced had smothered those butterflies.

Chapter Seven

Gabe held her door open and helped her get in and settled before closing the door tight and lapping the plane once. He hoped this was a wild experience for her. Knowing she was a little nervous, he'd decided to distract her with a kiss. Her lips had tasted delicious. She must have on some berry-flavored lip balm.

Gabe sat in his seat and locked his belt, showing her how to fasten hers. Holding out a pair of headphones to Holly, he said, "It's going to be really loud as soon as the engine comes on. We need to wear these so we can talk to each other."

Holly took the headphones from him, and they put them on at the same time. Gabe thought explaining each step might help with her nerves, so he shared each of his moves. "Okay, here's what I do each time, step by step. First, I make sure the parking brake is set. Next, that the circuit breakers are all in and the avionics master switch is off." He looked over and saw her nod, her eyes intent on his every move.

Gabe loved going through these steps. After the number of years he'd been doing this, he never felt like it was rote and that he could do it in his sleep. He took every flight as seriously as the last, never wanting to come off as cocky and something go terribly wrong because he missed a step.

"Next I check the fuel and the throttle settings." Turning on the master switch came after that. "This primes the engine," he said, pumping the handle. "And this switch flips on the beacon light."

Gabe checked on her again and saw was looking at the instrument panel with wide eyes. Her bobbing knee caught his attention, her nerves likely getting the better of her. When she noticed him looking at her, she gave him a wobbly grin. And a thumbs up. Gabe pulled the mic down in front of his lips and said, "Speak into the mic and let's make sure it works."

Holly reached up and followed his lead, pulling the mic into place. "I can hear you just fine."

"I've got to yell out my window now to clear the prop before we turn on the engine. I just wanted to give you a heads up." Holly gave him a thumbs up again.

Gabe cracked open the window and yelled, "Clear prop!" There shouldn't be anyone out there right now, but he had to do it to warn anyone around the plane that the engine was about to start. Gabe turned the key and the engine roared to life. He loved that loud purr. The propeller began spinning and Gabe could feel the vibrations in his seat.

The oil pressure gauge was in the green and the navigation lights were on. He flipped the avionics master switch and made sure the radios were on. The final pre-flight check list item was to take the flaps up.

Gabe smiled at Holly. She still looked a little anxious, her eyes bright and wide. "All done. Are you ready?" When she nodded, he added, "If you feel sick at any time let me know. Barf bags are in that compartment," he said, reaching across her lap to pull open the door, showing her rather than just telling. "But you're not going to need one. Promise."

"I appreciate your confidence."

Gabe nodded. "Now let's go see the sun dip behind the hilltops." Pulling out his phone he opened his camera app and turned it to selfie mode. Holding it aloft, he leaned his head towards hers. Both had glowing smiles when he snapped the pic. Reaching over he slid his hand along her shoulder, then between her hair and neck, giving it a squeeze. "Oh, one more thing. Kiss me for luck."

Holly's eyes seemed to blaze as her stare captured his. Then her eyes drifted to his mouth, and she moved closer. Gabe shifted his mic first then hers out of the way so their path was unencumbered. Their lips collided and he felt the jolt. It hit him in the gut and radiated outward from there. His hand tensed on the back of her neck, wanting to pull her closer, maybe even all the way over into his lap. But he forced his fingers to relax, to let go.

Not the time or the place for that. Damn Ryan for putting thoughts about the mile-high club in his head.

Holly blinked her eyes when he pulled back, disengaging his lips from hers. That kiss was even hotter than the last one. Drawing in a deep breath, he dropped his hand back to his lap and released the breath slowly. Shaking his shoulders as if a chill just raced down his spine, he tried to focus his mind once again.

Holly laughed and put her hand on top of his, squeezing his fingers. "I don't think you need any luck. But thanks again for trying to distract me."

"Anytime." Gabe winked, loving when her dimples winked back in reaction.

Gabe began the process of accelerating the plane toward the runway. He checked in with the tower and made plans to get them in the air.

Glancing once more at Holly, he was pleased to see that she seemed okay. She might be sitting on her hands though. Guess she was trying to hide her nerves. "Thank you for letting me talk you into going up with me."

Holly grinned but didn't take her gaze off the front windshield. He left her to preparing herself and got them moving.

Gabe loved that feeling of lift off. When the sensation of his stomach rising in his body took over. Some people hated that. He hoped Holly wasn't one of them.

Gabe decided he should probably continue to speak. Maybe that would be comforting. He kept up a steady stream, explaining about what each of the gauges were and what he was looking for. He told her about the speed they were going and the exact second that they left the ground. He had her focus on the sun straight ahead of them instead of the ground falling away.

The orange ball was nestled in the valley between two peaks. They were up in the air at just the right moment to see it sink behind the ground.

"Pretty," Holly exclaimed. He noticed her hands were in her lap now, so he hoped that meant she was feeling less nervous. "The pinks and oranges are gorgeous."

"And behind us the sky should already be turning navy-blue. We'll see stars popping out soon."

"This is beautiful, Gabe." There was a sound of awe in her voice, and he liked that he had a hand in putting it there. He wasn't responsible for the sky's colors, but he'd gotten her here to see it up close. "Thank you so much for bringing me up here."

"You're welcome." Gabe pointed. "Look, there's some lights off to your side."

Holly peered out her side window at the neighborhood below. Gabe looked out his side spotting more to show her. He headed west another twenty minutes before making the turn back to the south, flying into a deep purple sky.

"The town looks amazing from up here!" Holly's smile was just as bright as the lights below. Asking her to do this had been completely spur of the moment and giving her the reason of seeing the lights from above had just been him pulling something out of his ass so she'd commit. "Is that Santa's Village?" she exclaimed, pointing straight ahead.

"It is," Gabe confirmed.

"It looks so magical." Wistfulness colored her voice.

"Since you're up here with me, who's filling in for you down there?"

"My brother. It was his turn for a shift. But he's seventeen and thinks being an elf is one of *the most* embarrassing things on the planet. He's not wrong," she added, shaking her head.

Gabe looked over at her and asked, "How many siblings do you have?"

"Four. I'm the oldest."

"Wow!" he exclaimed. "That's a lot."

Holly laughed. "Yes, it is. We are quite a loud bunch when we all get together. Chris ranks as the youngest and the only boy, so he has had a hard life." She rolled her eyes and Gabe smiled. But that smile quickly dropped when she asked, "Do you have any siblings?"

He should have known it was coming. But the words still sent a shockwave through his heart. Pulling in a deep breath, he wondered if he should give her the public version or the truth? Gabe debated as the sound of the engine roared beyond his headphones. Then in a flash he realized where better to have this conversation, but in the air, his favorite place to be.

Plus, he didn't have to look her in the eyes while he shared about some of the worst times of his life.

"No," Gabe finally said and saw out of the corner of his eye her shoulders drop. His delay had probably caused her to think she'd upset him by asking. "My mom was young when she had me. I have no idea who my sperm donor is. She never told me." Gabe shrugged, like it didn't bother him. He hadn't thought about it in years, so maybe that was true.

Keeping his head on a swivel and his eyes locked on the world outside the windows, he watched for anything that might interfere with their flight. He could feel her eyes on him but accepted it as comforting rather than judging.

"We didn't have much growing up. Moving around a lot kept us from accumulating anything. She never mentioned any family, and I didn't ask her. I just tried to be a good kid, keep to myself, and take care of her anyway I could."

Now came the hardest part. The words he'd never spoken aloud to anyone. "She died on my tenth birthday."

Holly's hand slid across his thigh, squeezing, the pressure comforting. He covered her hand with his, lacing their fingers.

"She'd been sick. Since she didn't have a job with insurance, she never went to the doctor. I don't even know what she had. I was placed into the foster care system and bounced around from house to house. I wasn't a bad kid, just one that didn't communicate well."

"You were traumatized, Gabe. That's to be expected," Holly added, her voice soothing in the headphones.

Gabe let his eyes focus on the glowing lights from the ground for a few moments before continuing his vigilance. "Whenever Christmas time came around, I always got sent back, due to lack of money, or them wanting to only spend it on their own kids. I'm not really sure what their reasons were, I just know that I never spent a Christmas with any of the families I lived with." The familiar sadness pressed down on him, but then an amazing thing happened. That heavy weight started to shift, sliding away from his heart. Not completely but talking about it was breaking up that solid plaster of pain surrounding it.

He had to blink his eyes twice to clear them before continuing, his focus going back to the sky beyond the windshield. "I aged out of foster care with nowhere to go and no interest in going to college. So I immediately enlisted. I figured I could find a family of brothers in the Marine Corps."

Gabe took another deep breath as he felt his body changing. *Look at that.* The child psychologists he'd been forced to see when he first entered foster care had been right after all. Saying all of that out loud must be cathartic because he felt lighter. If anyone asked him to explain *how* he felt lighter, he didn't think he could. But that was the word that came to mind.

Curious to know her reaction to his verbal vomit, he glanced over. Holly's eyes glistened with unshed tears. Her lips trembled and he knew she was trying to hold in her tears for him.

"You don't have to cry for me, Holly. But don't hold 'em back either," he added, unlinking his hand from hers, using the side of his finger to catch the tears that overflowed her eyelashes.

"I'm so sorry you had to go through all that." She sniffed, her voice scratchy. Like she'd been holding back those tears for a while. "I'm so sorry about your mom and all the uncertainty that followed."

Gabe let all that settle in before he decided he needed to lighten the mood. He forced a grin and asked, "How's that for heavy, first-date, getting-to-know-you material?"

Holly's laugh came out more like a snort and she wiped her cheeks then her nose with the back of her gloved hand. "Ugh. Got any tissues in this rig?"

Gabe's lips lifted, shifting into a smile as he reached behind his seat and grabbed a roll of paper towels. He held it out and she pulled off a sheet. "Thank you." She wiped her face and nose again, blinking her eyes rapidly. "And thank you for sharing that with me. Now I can see why you're not a fan of Christmas."

"My reasons may be legit, but I'm realizing that it's time to let go of all that anger, sadness, and frustration." He turned towards her and this time his grin wasn't forced. "I live in Tinsel, Tennessee now for God's sake. I'm not going to be able to get away from it."

Chapter Eight

"Wooohoooo!" Holly let out the biggest, most surprising yell when the wheels touched down with a little bounce on the runway. "That was incredible!" She knew she was yelling into the mic, but she couldn't help it. The rush that was flooding through her veins right now couldn't be described with words. Her heart was slamming into her ribs, and her lungs were working overtime.

Gabe looked over at her and the smile on his face was the biggest she'd ever seen. Granted she hadn't known him long, but she had seen his lips curve upward a time or two. But this smile, this smile was exhilarating, or maybe that was just the high she was feeling from experiencing a plane landing with a bird's eye view of the whole process.

Gabe brought the plane back toward the hangar. After braking, he went through what must be a well-practiced routine to shut everything down. She watched as his long-fingered hands set everything to rights. Then he grabbed his headphones and removed them.

Holly couldn't stop staring at him. He'd been so capable, so confident, so incredibly sexy in his element. She was having trouble catching her breath. She'd never felt anything like it before.

Gabe unclipped his seatbelt, then reached over and lifted her headphones off her head. He hung both sets up on the dash then turned in his seat to face her. He smoothed the hair down that had been lifted by the headphones, sliding it behind her ears, tapping a candy cane dangling from her earlobe. Holly felt multiple tingles begin to radiate out from where his warm skin touched hers. Then he just stared at her, his gorgeous green eyes bright in the lights from above, shifting from hers to her lips.

Yes, *please.*

She wanted to kiss him. Needed to kiss him. So much had just happened over the last hour or so. Her nervous system was on overdrive, from seeing all those beautiful colors of the sunset, to the lights below, to him sharing about his past.

Then the best part, the absolute rush of the landing at the end.

Holly reached up and put her hands on his cheeks, pulling him toward her. Because she hadn't undone her seatbelt, she was trapped. The second his lips touched hers, her eyes closed, and she let his scent and heat surround her, absorbing them into her skin. Her hands slid around his head through his buzzed hair, gripping, desperate to get closer to him. Gabe's tongue touched her lips, and they parted, welcoming him.

Holly heard the click of metal and realized he'd freed her from the restraint of her belt. She immediately pushed up and turned toward him. His hands were beneath her legs, lifting, moving her to straddle him. He caressed her ass before sliding his hands along the tops of her thighs as she lowered herself to sit on his lap. Her mouth gravitated back to his like a homing beacon. Heat radiated off him, warming her, and she pressed against his body. Wrapping her arms around his broad shoulders, she leaned all the way in.

This kiss was epic. She hungered for him. Couldn't get enough. Her hips, without her permission, started rocking against him.

Gabe released her lips and mumbled against her skin as he kissed along her jaw and neck, "Holly, this is likely just the product of the adrenaline flowing through you and I'm all for it, but—" He broke off to nuzzle the swinging candy cane. A shiver skated across her skin when he nipped her earlobe. "But, don't do anything you wouldn't have done an hour ago." Gabe threaded his fingers through her hair and leaned back to look into her eyes.

Holly's breath panted in and out. She tried to steady her breathing so she could concentrate on what he was saying.

"I get what it feels like to experience what you just did. The adrenaline rush I felt at going Mach 2 for the first time was the most intense thing I've ever experienced. I was hooked from that moment on."

Holly couldn't even imagine what that would be like. But the intensity she felt buzzing off his body was addictive.

"I'm an adrenaline junkie," he continued, his eyes laser-focused on hers. "I live for this stuff. I love that you loved it too. You were too distracted to be nervous, weren't you?"

Holly nodded. She also shifted up off his legs slightly because she'd felt the change in the air. The pull back. The reset. "I was. It was amazing up there." *I can't wait to do it again.* But she didn't want to put that out there. This was just a first date. A first date and here she was straddling the man in the cockpit of his plane, practically devouring him. "But you're right. I think I am feeling an adrenaline overload right now."

"There are many ways that you can burn off that energy. This is one way," he added, his hands drifting down her arms to her thighs, where his fingers pressed deeply into her skin, like a massage. His thumbs skated along her inner thighs, dangerously close to bringing her an immense amount of pleasure. "Or we could go for a run."

That brought her out of her lust-filled haze. "It's like thirty degrees outside. Plus, running's not my thing."

Gabe shrugged like that was no big deal for him. "Okay, then, how about yoga?"

Holly quirked an eyebrow. "You do yoga?" She realized her breathing was nearly back to normal. Him cutting them off when he did was a good decision. And he was right, adrenaline was definitely fueling this escapade. She wasn't normally this bold on a first date. But there was something about Gabe Shepherd that drew her in. Whether it was his voice, his beautiful green eyes, or the need to comfort him because of his dislike for the holiday season, she didn't know.

But what she did know was that she was going to have this man for dessert. It could be tonight, or it might be next week, but she was getting herself a helping of Gabe Shepherd.

***

"I have beer, wine, soda. What's your pleasure?" Holly called out from the kitchen.

That was a loaded question. *What's your pleasure?* Since he was coming off his own adrenaline high, he'd love to have her. Naked and under him. Right here on this couch. Or on the bed, whichever she preferred.

Gabe cleared his mind and his throat before saying, "Beer sounds good."

Holly had suggested they come to her house for dinner. She'd had all the makings for her famous tortilla soup ready to put in the pot. He'd liked the idea of a homecooked meal and more time alone with her, so here they were.

He'd offered to help but she'd pushed him out of the kitchen and told him to sit and relax. Relaxing was a bit of a stretch since he still had so much pent-up energy rolling through his veins, but he was trying.

Her house was about the size of the one he was renting, but it held way more personal items than his did. There were photos everywhere. He guessed most were of her siblings. It looked like they all shared the dimple trait.

She'd tapped a button when they'd come inside, and a fire had ignited in the gas fireplace. His eyes were drawn to the motion of the flames. Seeing the mantel above it bare surprised him. Same with the tree sitting beside it. For all her Christmasy persona, he'd have figured the inside of her house would be just as decked out as the outside.

Two plastic tubs sat next to the tree. The lids were locked on tight. Not a single ornament graced the branches. He motioned to them when Holly stepped back through the doorway bringing him a bottle of beer. "Is there a tradition of waiting until a certain day to decorate?"

He accepted the beer she held out to him and shifted when she tucked a leg under her and sat beside him on the couch. She tapped her open beer bottle to the neck of his and sighed. "I'm only waiting until I have the energy to do it. I'm feeling a little stretched thin this Christmas."

Gabe shifted his arm along the back of the couch, resting his hand on her shoulder. His fingers started to dig into the tense muscles in her neck. The way she closed her eyes and sighed suggested that he keep up the action. "You have several jobs that keep you busy."

"Yeah, too busy on some days." Her eyes opened and her gaze drifted to the tree. Her expression turned sad. "My youngest sister told me a couple nights ago that I have the 'first-child syndrome.'"

Gabe grinned, curious. His hand continued to smooth out the muscles along her shoulders now. "I haven't heard of that."

Holly released a long breath and shook her head. "Taking on too much responsibility. Feeling the need to be and do all the things." She sighed then sipped her beer. "Guilty."

"I don't know from experience since I don't have any siblings but having a leadership role in the military might correlate some."

"Likely. I just need to learn to say no to things. And to delegate. I'm not needed at the roofing office all the time. And *Deck This House* is seasonal. Same with Santa's Village. But if I was to let one of those go, I think it would be the elf costume."

"I thought you looked sexy in it. When I first heard from Joseph that you and your siblings all dressed up as elves my mind went a whole different direction," he admitted with a wink.

She laughed, the sound doing something funny to his stomach. "A little more naughty list than nice?"

Gabe didn't answer, just grinned, the bottle held against his lips.

Holly stood up and started back for the kitchen. She paused in the doorway and looked over her shoulder, her dimples winking at him. "Oh, I have one of those too."

Gabe sputtered and nearly choked on the beer he'd just tried to swallow. Her laughter could be heard over his coughing. *Damn.* Getting to see that just moved to the top of his Christmas list. Actually it was the only thing on the list since making a Christmas wish list was new to him.

He set the bottle on the coffee table and stood up. Pulling a tissue from a box on the end table, he dabbed at the beer on his jeans. Wadding it up, he tossed it in the trash can beside the TV. Curiosity got the better of him and he popped the lid on both tubs next to the tree. She'd seemed so sad when she'd been looking at her bare tree. The least he could do was offer to help. Having never done this before he didn't know where to start.

The first thing he spotted was something that brought a twinkle to his eye. Lord, he was thinking like he was in a storybook. But the thoughts he was having about Holly in her naughty-list elf costume had no business being in any kids' books.

Glancing around he found the best place to hang it. There was already a nail above the doorway to the kitchen. Sliding the ribbon over the nail he moved back to the tubs and picked up the garland.

"So what goes on first? The garland or ornaments?"

His question was met with silence. He turned to face the kitchen door wondering if she'd heard him. He thought he could hear her working by the stove. Chopping and stirring.

Holly poked her head around the doorframe, her eyebrow quirked in question.

Gabe held up the garland and a snowman on a string. "Which one goes first?"

"You've never decorated a tree before?"

Gabe's head tilted and he returned her quirked-eyebrow look.

"Oh, right. Sorry." She pointed to his left hand. "Um, the garland. But you don't have to do that. You don't even like Christmas."

True. But it was growing on him. Or maybe it was just her. "But I like helping. And you look like you could use some help."

"I'd like that." Her smile grew and she added, "Tonight will be a night of firsts for both of us.

But wait for me. The soup is almost ready. We can eat first then decorate."

Gabe set the items he was holding down on the coffee table and motioned above her.

When she glanced up her dimples were on full display.

He moved toward her, and Holly stood tall beneath the mistletoe. As soon as he got touching-close she went up on her toes and wrapped her arms around his shoulders. He slid his hands along her sides and around her back drawing her in. "Tonight will be a night of firsts for both of us," he repeated, his words whispered in the narrow space between their mouths. Then his lips took hers.

No gentle press.

No teasing touches.

Just simply took.

He tasted salt from something she'd added to the soup, likely nibbling while she prepared it. Lapping it up, he slid his tongue between her lips and stroked it across hers. His breath caught when she leaped up, wrapping her legs around his hips. Grabbing her ass, he pulled her even closer, his dick eager to be inside her.

A beeping sound could be heard over the rush of blood pounding through his ears. Sighing against her mouth, he shifted, settling his lips against the crook of her neck and shoulder. He couldn't resist licking her skin, needing a moment to come off this high, before helping set her feet back on the ground.

She shivered in reaction and groaned. He felt the same. They both seemed to release each other at the same time. His hands guided her, keeping their bodies connected as she slid to the floor. The feeling of her soft breasts gliding over his chest made him want to crush the timer in his bare hands.

Chapter Nine

Dinner before dessert. Dinner before dessert. Holly repeated that in her head as she slid down Gabe's deliciously hard body. She'd been set ablaze by his lips, his hands, the hard evidence of his arousal pressing against her body.

Stepping back, she couldn't resist brushing her thumb over his full bottom lip. Nibbling on it some more was definitely on the menu for the night. The timer beeped again, and she pushed off his hard chest, forcing herself to step away. Taking a deep breath, she blew it out slowly.

In through the nose, out through the mouth.

Holly got two soup mugs out of the cupboard to the right of the stove. She spooned a heaping helping into both bowls and set them on her large plates. Around each plate she added tortilla chips and crackers. Dropping a large soup spoon into each bowl, she then wiped her hands on the towel hanging from the oven door. She double checked the timer and burner were off before carrying the tray of food into the living room.

Gabe sat on the couch with his eyes focused on the flames until she walked in. Then his smoldery green gaze locked on hers. She set the tray on the coffee table and asked, "Would you like another beer?"

Gabe shook his head. "No thanks. Come and sit." He shifted forward on the couch, his elbows resting on his knees and pulled in a breath through his nose. "That smells delicious." Holly handed him a plate and tossed a green cloth napkin covered in angels over his thigh before sitting beside him.

"The angel Gabriel," she muttered. Holly tilted her head, realizing she hadn't put the two together until now. "And Shepherd. Wow. And you thought I have a Christmasy name."

Gabe looked over at her, his lips twisting. "Kinda ironic, isn't it?"

"Both of us with Christmasy names living in a Christmasy town. What are the odds?"

"Completely off the charts." Gabe took a bite of his soup and nodded his head. "Delicious." He ate another bite before returning to the topic. "But my mother grew up here. She must have had a reason for my first name."

"You mentioned Joseph earlier. Is that Joseph Shepherd? Are you related?" Holly stirred in some tortilla strips and took a bite. Her tastebuds did a happy dance. She loved this soup and was happy to see Gabe enjoying it too. She wasn't much of a cook, but she had a couple recipes she did well. And did on repeat.

Holly looked at him when he didn't respond right away. He stared straight ahead, his eyes appearing unfocused on the flames, and his mouth looked tense. Was he uncomfortable? "You don't have to answer," she rushed to say. "The name just made me curious. My grandfather worked with Joseph Shepherd at the Chevy Plant. They are such good friends that they have coffee together nearly every morning at Ralph's Diner."

Gabe swallowed his bite then set his plate down. His gaze remained focused in front of them. She watched his hands come together between his knees, fingers clenching into fists. "Last year I received an email from a man named Joseph Shepherd. A name I didn't recognize." Gabe's head turned and his gaze zeroed in on hers, the intensity unexpected. "He told me he was my grandfather. That my mother was his daughter. That after *her* mother had died, she'd run away from home when she was sixteen and he had no idea I existed." Gabe stopped and swallowed hard. "Until he'd done a DNA test kit and found me that way."

Wow, how unreal. She couldn't imagine how he must have felt in that moment. Having his mom die when he was so young and not belonging to anyone for years had to be heartbreaking. Then to find out he did have family. A good man too. Holly released a slow, silent breath. One she'd been holding since he'd first spoken about the email. "Last year?"

Gabe nodded, his eyes on the flames once again. "I was still in Afghanistan, active duty. It blew me away. I told you my mom never mentioned any family, and I never asked."

"Joseph is a wonderful man." Holly reached over, sliding her hand into his, cupping his palm. The tenseness went out of it immediately. He flexed his fingers then laced them with hers. "It's a miracle he found you."

"A Christmas miracle," he muttered.

Holly thought Gabe needed a change of scene to help shift from this heavy conversation. "Another Christmas miracle? You getting to decorate a tree for the first time. How about it?" She stood and pulled on their joined hands, encouraging him to rise, to say yes. "It'll be fun. I won't turn on the Christmas music because that might be too much for you, but just know that's how I usually do it. The fireplace lit, the music soft in the background, a steaming mug of hot chocolate nearby."

Gabe rose and pulled her into his arms. "Thank you," he whispered against her ear. His breath moving the candy cane dangling there, tickling her oversensitive skin.

Holly didn't speak. She didn't think she needed to. She just held him tight and waited for him to take all the hug that he needed. Spending time in his arms, pressed against his hard, hot body was fine by her. She could stay here all night.

And hopefully, she will be in this same position later tonight. Just minus the clothes.

Gabe slowly released her, and she moved over to the tubs on the floor. Reaching in she removed all the garland she had. Most of the strands were red and gold mixed together. She handed him one end. "I like to start at the top. Tuck it in around the middle near that top branch," she instructed, pointing. "This is the first year I won't need a ladder."

Gabe chuckled as he stretched his arm overhead and placed the garland securely near the top. Holly glanced down at the smooth skin exposed below his sweater caused by his overhead stretch. The sight of fine hairs on tan skin brought her butterfly friends back. Biting her lip, she tried to bring her focus back to the task at hand and said, "Now wrap it around the back. I'll do the front part then hand it back to you." They worked together to string the garland around the tree, until the final piece curved around the bottom branches.

"What's next?"

"The lights." Holly pulled out the roll of lights and handed it to him. "This also starts at the top and winds around on a track similar to the garland."

Holly watched him closely and thought he looked like he might be enjoying himself. She didn't want to ask. She didn't want him to have to voice how he was feeling. No pushing. Not from her. She just enjoyed seeing him in the moment. Doing something he'd never done before.

This was her thirty-third Christmas. Minus those first couple of years, she'd been doing this each season. It was something that she looked forward to. Seeing all the old ornaments from her childhood. New ones that she'd made at art classes she took with her sisters or friends. Her tree was eclectic, just the way she liked it. No rhyme or reason to the decorations. She'd never been one of those all-white-lights kind of gals. She thrived on color.

"Am I doing this right?"

His voice startled her, bringing her out of her reverie. She'd never heard that tone before. It was the least confident she'd heard his voice to date. "Absolutely. Here, once we get to this spot, we need to connect the next string." She did so then passed the next spool to him to wrap about the backside.

Gabe suddenly turned a smile on her. She paused, her arms outstretched for the spool. Her lips slowly curved, knowing in her heart that he was indeed enjoying this moment. She was so happy that she could be here to see it.

"Now it's time for the ornaments. You might see some that are made of popsicle sticks or yarn. Just know those were made when I was probably four or five, so no judging." She moved the tub of ornaments onto the coffee table for easier reach. Pulling out a blue bulb, she spun it in her hands. Her name was painted on it in gold letters. "My grandma made this for me. She made each of us one when we were born. The year I moved out, my mom had this in a box of things for me to take when I set out on my own."

"That's special." He glanced back at the tree. "Do you have a certain place you like to hang any of these?"

Holly shook her head. She did, but she wasn't going to tell him that and give him a reason to bow out. She wanted him to have the experience of hanging ornaments on a Christmas tree. Besides, tonight was a night of firsts, right? This could be the first of many years that Christmas was done differently in this house. "I change it up each year. Put them wherever you'd like."

Gabe pulled out three clear glass reindeer and carefully hung them from different branches. "Put on the music. You know you're missing it. I promise it won't hurt me."

Holly side-eyed him as she looped a ceramic snowman on the lowest branch.

"I promise. Do it, Holly. You know you want to," he crooned, his voice deep and low.

She didn't want to put him out, but she definitely was missing it. She usually sang along and sipped her hot chocolate. Maybe she still could. "Okay, I'll be right back."

Holly left the room and asked her smart speaker to play traditional Christmas music while she turned on the burner to heat water for her hot chocolate. She added the ingredients to her mug, this one boasting an elf with a twinkle in her eye and a mischievous smile on her red lips. Holly felt like she was channeling that elf right now. She was feeling a little mischievous, thinking about exactly which drawer her sexy elf negligee was in.

Maybe she'd be sporting it soon.

Bing Crosby sung about a white Christmas. She poured in the hot water then reentered the living room stirring her mix with a peppermint stick. She saw him eyeing her mug as she brought it to her lips for a sip. "I've got more water heated if you'd like me to make you a cup."

Gabe waved her off. "I'm good, thank you. I want you to enjoy it." His fingertip brushed the side of her mug, right over the elf's grin. "Nice."

"I thought it was appropriate." Holly sipped, then feeling a little naughty, pulled the peppermint stick from the frothy chocolate and licked the chocolate off the length of it before slurping it into her mouth. She held in the giggle when she watched his throat work, his Adam's apple bobbing. He surprised her when he took the mug from her hand and set it on the mantel behind her. Taking the peppermint stick from her mouth he took his own lick before tossing it back in the mug. They stood staring at each other. Holly's heart thumped wildly in her chest, her butterflies doing flips in her belly.

"All I want for Christmas is...."

Holly tuned in and realized Mariah Carey was singing those words. "What do you want for Christmas, Gabe?"

Chapter Ten

There was no hesitation on his part. "To see Holly in her naughty-list elf costume."

She swallowed. Her breath becoming choppy. "It's less of a costume and more of a silky—"

Her words were cut off by his lips. Gabe's mouth consumed hers. Strong hands roamed through her hair, across her back, then under her thighs, lifting her. Holly quickly twined her legs around his hips, back in the position she'd put herself in earlier. Back where she wanted to be with her hands gripping his powerful shoulders, her nails sinking into the fabric of his thin sweater.

Gabe turned them, not taking his mouth off hers. He only stumbled once on some packing that had been around the ornaments. Holly mumbled against his mouth, "First door. Right side." She flipped the bathroom light switch on when they passed by. It was enough light to illuminate her bed. Gabe carried her to it, then suddenly she was falling. She bounced when she landed on the bed. Gabe reached down and pulled off her boots and socks. She started to reach for the snap of her jeans, but he stopped her. "Let me."

Her hands fell back to the bed, limp. But her fingers curled into the comforter when his hands slid up her legs, stroking her thighs as they moved to her hips. His fingertips danced along the bare skin at her waistline. Tingling sensations sparked along the trail he made. The sound of the snap popping and the zipper hissing was loud in the room. She could still hear the carols, but mostly she was focused on the man before her, slowly undressing her. Holly raised her hips and helped him shimmy her jeans down her legs.

She couldn't take it any longer. Sitting up she drew her sweater over her head and tossed it to the floor. Gabe took a moment to do the same to his. Holly rose to her knees and moved closer to the edge of the bed, needing to touch him. His chest was solid, his abs strong. Short, dark hairs covered his pecs and created a trail for her nails to follow down the center of his chest to his navel. His muscles rippled beneath her touch.

Holly felt zero nerves kneeling before him in only her bra and panties. The heat from his gaze only gave her more courage to reach for his snap and zipper. Gabe's hands came to rest on her sides, his thumbs caressing her beaded nipples through the fabric of her bra. Holly needed a moment to breathe through that sensation before continuing with her task of removing his jeans.

She pushed them down his hips and thighs. Gabe stepped out of his jeans, kicking them aside. His boxer briefs molded to his skin, tenting in the front.

"Holly, you are so beautiful." His voice quiet, his words gravelly. "I need to touch you."

"I need you to touch me," she whispered back. And she wanted to touch him, so she did. Her hand slid past the waistband of his boxer briefs and she gripped his length. Gabe growled and yanked his underwear down. He pushed Holly back on the bed and followed her down, shifting until he was resting between her thighs. She spread her legs wider allowing him to get closer.

"I thought you wanted to see me in my silky elf suit—"

"It's not Christmas yet," he said against her neck. "Next time. I need you too much to wait another minute." Gabe's mouth left a scorching hot trail down her neck, nipping at her shoulder before crossing over to her breast. His hands moved to her back, pulling the clasp of her bra apart, then sliding the straps down her arms. He focused on all the skin he was uncovering. The second her nipples were exposed his mouth covered one, his hand the other.

The pull from his mouth had electricity shooting from her nipples straight to her sex. If she wasn't already wet, she certainly was now.

Wet and ready. Holly reached down and took him in hand once again. His skin was hot yet smooth beneath her roving fingertips. She felt the moan rumble from deep in his chest at the movement of her hand stroking him.

"I won't last a minute if you keep that up," he grumbled against her other breast. Gabe pulled back out of her reach and slid down her body, taking her panties with him. He spread her thighs with his broad shoulders and Holly's heart triple-timed when his mouth touched her sex. He went right for the heart of her, teasing her clit with flicks of his tongue. Holly's hips rose on their own accord, pushing herself closer to that teasing tongue. Gabe's hands reached up and held her hips down against the bed, keeping her from rising too far.

Holly used her hands instead, gripping his head, pushing him, holding him in place as the sensations built up inside her. Gabe slid a finger into her heat, and her muscles clenched around him. In and out he stroked, and all she could think about was his dick doing the same, stretching her, filling her. Holly knew she was close, the tide rising inside her. She spread her legs out wider, needing him to push harder.

Suddenly he pulled back and his eyes met hers. Holly groaned at his absence. Before she knew what was happening, Gabe had switched positions with him on his back. "Come here, baby." He pulled on her hands, drawing her towards him. "Have a seat. I know you want to move." He gripped her hips and pulled her into position with her knees beside his shoulders.

Holly hesitated. "You want me to—"

"Yep, sit on my face, baby, I need to make you come."

And Holly needed to come. She'd been so close. Just the thought of sitting like this, with her heat directly over his face caused her to start dripping. Taking a deep breath, she spread her knees wider. She didn't know what to do with her hands, lifting them, then dropping them to her sides.

"Grab on to the wall, baby." She did.

His gravelly voice, his words, the hard lick of his tongue brought her back to the brink instantly.

Stroking her ass, he pressed deep into her muscles before sliding a hand forward. He pushed one finger into her, then two, stretching her. Holly held her breath as the orgasm blasted through her, rippling along her nerves.

"Don't hold it in, baby. I want to hear you."

Holly released her pent-up breath and moaned out his name. "Oh my God, oh my Gabe, that was...you...holy shit."

Gabe chuckled against her thigh and she thought she might explode again. She'd never had an orgasm as intense as that one. Never. She had no idea when her heart would ever resume its natural rhythm, forever altered by this man below her. The man who was currently grinning up at her from between her thighs.

Holly fell back on top of him, twisting her legs to the side to get her ass out of his face. She flopped her arms out to the side, her cheek resting on his stomach. His pulse thumped as rapidly as hers. Gabe's right arm came up to cover her legs, his hand stroking her overly sensitive skin. His hand dipped between her thighs and Holly was surprised that she was ready. Ready for his touch. Ready for another orgasm. Ready for this man to be inside her.

His fingers slid over her wetness. "Holly, you're so wet."

"You did that to me." She kissed his hard abs and rose. "Now I'm ready for you." Holly settled herself back on top of him, this time straddling his hips.

"Condom," he grumbled, moving to reach over the side of the bed.

"I have some. In that drawer right there."

Gabe eyed her, probably thinking about her past sex partners. She hadn't had many. But she did believe in being prepared. "I used to be a girl scout. Be prepared."

Gabe pulled the drawer open. She rubbed herself against his hot, hard length, her sex clenching in anticipation while he struggled to rip open the box.

Finally, Gabe had the foil packet open and he pulled her head down for a kiss before donning the condom.

Holly shifted so she could guide him inside. Her wetness made for a smooth entrance. They both groaned at the contact. Holly closed her eyes and leaned back, her hair sliding around her shoulders. Gabe's hands gripped her hips. She lifted them, loving the feel of him sliding inside her, then sank back down on him. Gabe helped her keep a steady rhythm. Holly's nails dug into his pecs as she rode him.

When he leaned up and pulled a nipple into his mouth, rolling his tongue around it, tweaking it with his teeth, she was unprepared for the strength of this second orgasm that took her breath.

Her orgasm sent him over the edge and he cried out her name as he pulled her down to take her mouth. His hips pistoned into her and she met every thrust, over and over until he released her mouth, winded, his breath coming out in pants.

"Damn, woman, that about killed me."

Holly laid flat over his chest, chuckling, thinking she couldn't have said it better.

***

Gabe pulled the blanket up over Holly after she'd joined him on the couch. She'd reheated their soup and they'd enjoyed it standing by the stove in the kitchen, ravenous. Next, they put the remaining ornaments on the tree and added the finishing touch—sprinkling tinsel all over the branches. Now with their stomachs full and their hearts happy, they lay satiated on the couch, enjoying the dancing light from the flames and the twinkling glow of the lights on the Christmas tree.

"Was decorating the tree everything you thought it would be?"

Her voice was quiet but he heard her clearly in the silence of the room. His chest rose and fell with his deep breath. *Had it been?* As a kid he'd imagined adding lights and ornaments with his mom, smiling and singing carols along with her. He'd seen the TV shows and the movies. He'd known how it was supposed to be. But he never once got to experience it himself.

Until tonight.

Until he'd stepped out of his comfort zone and made the decision to help Holly. And in turn going through those motions had helped him as well. Lightened his heart, filled it with happiness rather than hurt and regret.

"I always imagined doing that with my mom. Or even being a bystander at one of my foster homes. But it never happened. Tonight," he started then faltered, moving his chin to rest on top of her head. "Tonight, my heart is full."

Holly snaked her hand out from under the blanket and brought it to rest against his cheek. He knew the scruff on his jaw had to scrape against her soft skin, but she didn't complain. Leaning up, she placed a gentle kiss on his lips. When she pulled back the firelight reflected in her wet eyes. "No tears, baby. Not for me.

I'm going to learn to let go of all that from my past and move forward. From today on. Today you showed me what I've been missing. With each ornament we hung up, I felt different. So thank you." His lips melted into hers, deepening, hoping to express his thanks through his kiss. Lifting his head, he used his thumb to wipe a tear trailing down her cheek.

Her voice was husky when she whispered, "You're welcome." Her eyes held his, her focus intent. Then her dimples flashed. "I get to decorate a country music star's house tomorrow."

He appreciated the change in topic. "Who is it?"

"Rebecca Ingraham. She's been away on tour and will be home for the holidays."

Gabe nodded. "I've heard of her. She's played overseas for the military."

"A hometown hero in her own rights."

"I imagine her house is large. Do you have any help?" he asked, raising an eyebrow in question.

"Yes, two of my sisters and a guy who works for the roofing company. My dad even said he'd stop by. I think that they are more star-struck than willing to help, but I'll take it."

"How do you decorate a two-story house?"

"Very carefully," she quipped, resting her face against his chest, snuggling under the covers once again. "Tall ladders and harnesses. If only you had a helicopter, you could lower me down."

"If I had one."

"Well, maybe you can come by tomorrow and help. Or at least supervise."

Gabe rested his chin on top of her head. "I wish I could. But I have a meeting with Amos Tucker. By noon tomorrow I'll be the owner of a flying lessons business."

Holly pulled back, tilting her head up to meet his gaze. "Wow. That's amazing. You're going to be a great instructor. Guess that means you'll be sticking around."

Guess so. Gabe hadn't realized it but he'd starting growing roots in this crazy-ass town. It was starting to grow on him. And so was she. Gabe wrapped his arms tighter around her. His gaze lost focus in the flames as he thought about how much his life had changed in the last forty-eight hours. Holly had brought so much light and joy to his world. He couldn't imagine going back to living each day the way he had before meeting her.

He hoped he wouldn't have to.

Chapter Eleven

Holly woke to the feeling of someone watching her. She didn't open her eyes yet but took stock of the scene around her. She knew she was in her bed, recognizing the scent and softness of her sheets. After making out on the couch last night, they'd stumbled back to her bed around midnight. After upping her orgasm count by two they collapsed in a tangle of arms and legs. She quickly fell into a deep, satiated sleep.

The light chest hairs tickled her cheek where her face rested over his heart. The thumping beat steady beneath her ear. The hand on his hard abs rose and fell with his breath. Her leg was draped across both of his. Holly was comfortable. More comfortable than she had been in her whole life.

Opening her eyes, she was surprised to see that it was still dark out. Tilting her head back she looked up to find Gabe's gaze locked on hers.

"Good morning, beautiful." His deep rumble sent a trail of shivers racing down her spine. His hand started caressing the bare skin along her back, moving up and down, warming her, thinking she was probably cold, when she was anything but.

"Good morning. Is it morning, or is it still nighttime?" Her eyes shifted to her window. Where the curtains parted, she could see dark sky.

"It's early. I've always been an early riser." He nuzzled the top of her head. "I'm sorry I woke you."

Holly yawned. "Were you watching me sleep?"

"No, just dreaming with my eyes open." His hand continued to rove up and down her back and she loved the sensation. The heat from his body was making her sleepy.

She blinked her eyes, looking up at him, knowing she needed to stay awake. "I hope they were good dreams."

Even in the darkness of her bedroom she could see his grin. "The best I've ever had."

Holly shifted her leg and accidentally bumped into him. "Oaf! Sorry."

Gabe moved his hand to settle on her knee, keeping her from another accidental brush.

"As payback for that, and since you're up early, how about we go for a run?" Gabe chuckled when she remained silent.

That sounded like a terrible idea. "Um, now? In the dark? In the cold?"

"I run every morning, no matter the weather. The cold is invigorating."

"That's dedication," she mumbled against his chest. Holly loved the results of his daily effort. Her hand moved over his chest and stomach, toned from that dedication. But she was thinking about a different way to exercise this morning. An activity that would elevate their heart rates and give them a good sweat.

But didn't involve getting out of bed.

Her hand slid further down his body until she touched him. Trailing her fingers along his length, she said, "Um, I'm going to have to think long and hard about your offer." Her fingers squeezed, emphasizing the words *long* and *hard*.

Gabe's groan at her first touch turned to a surprised laugh at her emphasized words. She felt the rumble against her cheek. His dick hardened beneath her delicate touch.

"Oh, I think I'm gonna need a raincheck. Something important just came up." This time she emphasized *up*.

"Wiseass," he laughed against her ear as he flipped them. Holly landed on her back with over two hundred pounds of pure muscle pressing down on her. She was in heaven. *Yes, please.*

Gabe raised up on his elbows and shifted until his *something important* found the juncture of her thighs. With one swift move he slid right in. After one long and slow thrust, he froze.

"Condom," he growled, his body tense.

Holly lay perfectly still even though her body wanted to squeeze him, welcoming him inside. She knew he was trying to hold back, to keep his body from moving. "I'm covered."

Gabe's gaze locked on hers. With his elbows planted on the bed, his fingers pushed the hair back off her forehead. "I've never—"

"Me either." Holly nodded, and her hands cupped his cheeks. "I'm covered. Besides—" she squirmed, squeezing her internal muscles, gripping him tight, "—you inside me, like this, is the best feeling—"

His kiss cut off her words. His tongue delved into her mouth, mimicking the rhythm of his dick. Gabe groaned her name into her open mouth. "I don't wanna come so soon. But this... it's so...and you're so tight..." Gabe's words faltered as he slid in and out of her. Holly's hands gripped his back muscles, hanging on for the wild ride. His hips tilted at just the right angle that lit up her clit. Sensations escalated.

Gabe moved a hand between their bodies and rubbed her sensitive bud, putting just the right amount of pressure that brought her so close. Holly arched her back, hoping to raise her breasts closer to his mouth. He took her hint and licked her nipple, drawing it into his mouth. When he nipped it between his teeth she exploded, crying out his name. "Oh, Gabe! Yes...that's just what I needed," she whispered against his ear when his mouth glided from her chest over her collarbone, nipping with his lips on the sensitive part of her neck.

Gabe brought his mouth back to hers, claiming it. His hips began to move, thrusting deeper, harder. Holly wrapped her legs around his hips, meeting each of his thrusts. She felt his muscles tighten as one just before his release.

Coming down off his high, Gabe's muscles relaxed, one by one, and he sank down, flush to her body, depleted. Gusts of hot air puffed against her neck where he'd buried his face. Holly closed her eyes and enjoyed every sensation radiating along her skin, from her toes to her elbows.

"Now that is the kind of exercise I can get behind every morning." Holly chuckled against his neck as she held him tight, pressing her heart to his.

She'd never had sex like this before.

This full-on, sensory overload that she just experienced with Gabe. Never before.

She couldn't believe how fast she was falling for him. Had she really only met him just over two days ago? It was amazing how fast her world could be flipped upside down from meeting one single human being. One human being out of millions that she could encounter, and this one changed her life irrevocably. This Christmas-hating man whose heart was full after sharing the experience of decorating her tree together.

This Marine pilot who stole her heart so quickly.

Maybe this was the year she'd get her Christmas wish.

***

Gabe unlocked his front door and stepped inside. He spotted Ryan in the kitchen guzzling a glass of water. He wore running shorts and sneakers, a black hoodie covering his top half. Sweat beaded his brow.

"Luuuceeee! You've got some 'splaining to do!"

Gabe tossed his keys on the kitchen island. He couldn't help the grin or the laugh that escaped. "You couldn't wait on me?"

Ryan raised his eyebrows. "Wait on you? I had no idea *when* or *if* you were coming home. I thought I was going to have to storm her little elf house and rescue you from your garland chains."

Gabe poured himself a glass of water and drank it down in one long swallow.

"Wow, you look like you're dehydrated. Guess you've already been exercising this morning. Is that a hickey on your neck?"

Gabe glared at him.

Ryan glared back. Then after a few seconds his lips split into a wide grin. "Happy for you, brother. What time's your meeting today?"

"Ten a.m. You coming with me?"

Ryan set his empty glass on the counter and shrugged. "Only to hang out in the background. You know, be your muscle. I'm not vouching for your character or anything."

Gabe scoffed. "Thanks, Ry."

"I'm just messing with you. Of course, I'm coming. I expect you to take me flying to celebrate."

Gabe caught his eye as he moved to refill his glass. "You know you can sign on now and have a stake in the business."

Ryan raised his hands, palms out. "Nah, man, that's your dream. I'm not horning in on it."

Gabe shook his head. Ryan looked sad. Defeated. He hadn't had a chance to ask him about Cheryl yet. But his buddy might not want to talk about it. Ryan had been thinking about retiring before the break-up. "When you retire, you can come fly with me. I'll need good pilots—"

It was Ryan's turn to scoff. "I'm better than good."

"And humble too," Gabe joked. "Hell, maybe you can even start a skydiving business alongside mine. We could go in together on that. I'll already have the planes. You'd just need to get the gear and the licensing." Gabe was warming up to this new idea. And from the look on Ryan's face, it had caught his attention. There was hope yet. "There'll always be a place here for you, Ry. Always."

***

"Aviation Training Academy officially has a new owner."

Gabe rose at the announcement from his lawyer. Amos did the same and reached across the conference table. Their hands shook, finalizing the human side of the business deal. Their lawyers would do the rest with all the legal jargon. Gabe was officially a business owner. Not having allowed himself to dream past his life in the Marines, he'd never pictured this for himself.

"Congratulations," Amos said, a grin on his wrinkled face.

"Same to you," Gabe commented. "Enjoy your retirement."

Amos nodded. "I will. It's a nice Christmas present for my wife. She's been on me for years about stepping away, being home more, traveling the country."

Gabe glanced at Ryan, who'd, as promised, hung in the background of the meeting. Gabe turned first to his lawyer and shook his hand. "Thank you, Curt."

"You're welcome, Gabe. I'll have everything to you by next week. Congratulations." Curt shook Amos's hand as well as his lawyer's before exiting the room, phone already at his ear.

Gabe met Ryan at the door and exited. Stepping out into the crisp, cold air, Gabe took in a deep breath. The air felt different. Smelled different. He felt different.

Ryan slapped him on the shoulder. "Congrats, buddy. I'm glad I'll have access to a plane now when I'm ready to zip off on that Caribbean vacay I've always dreamed of."

Gabe chuckled and led them over to the hangar that housed the Aviation Training Academy. The company's logo was emblazoned above the hangar doors. He stood back and took stock. This was all his now. The planes, the building, the team of mechanics, the admin staff, which actually only consisted of one woman who was in charge of scheduling and the books. Amos had expressed the need to keep her on because of her experience and knowledge of the business. Gabe thought nothing of it. He'd never replace a person who carried so much weight in the business. Alice was going to be his new best friend. He had a meeting scheduled with her after Christmas to work out the new arrangement.

Ryan suddenly spoke, drawing him out of his daydream. "Do you know what this business needs?"

Gabe gave him a quizzical look. "What's that?"

Ryan swung an arm around Gabe's neck and drew him in for a choke-hold hug. "A skydiving outfit."

Gabe hid his smile, looking over at the planes he now called his own. "You know," he said nodding his head, "I think you're right. You come up with that on your own?"

Ryan pushed him away. "No, some newly retired jackass who's trying to lure me in did."

"Did it work?"

Ryan stood with his hands on his hips, facing the hangar. "Consider me hooked."

"Did I hear you say skydiving?" The men turned at the question. Gabe was surprised to see his grandpa walking towards him across the tarmac.

"Joseph, what are you doing here?" Gabe reached out his hand for a handshake. Then, per their routine, Joseph took his hand and pulled him in for a hug, releasing his hand and wrapping his arms fully around him.

"Congratulations, son." Joseph squeezed his shoulders before stepping back. "I'm guessing the meeting was successful and you're looking over your newly acquired planes."

"Yes, sir. This here is the new owner of this fine establishment." Ryan stepped forward with his hand out. "Ryan Blaylock. Sir, it's an honor to meet you."

Joseph glanced between Gabe and Ryan then a smile lit up his face. "Ryan, Joseph Shepherd. It's a pleasure indeed. I've heard a lot about you."

Ryan started to speak, but Gabe cut him off. "Ahh, don't even ask if it was all good stuff. You know there's more ornery to you than nice," Gabe quickly said.

Ryan nodded and grinned. "True."

"What are you doing here?" Gabe asked again, not having expected to see him today.

"I'm here to celebrate with you."

A tingling feeling started somewhere around his heart and spread out with each rapid heart-beat. The feeling of support was foreign to him. He could only stare at the man who was his flesh and blood. Into green eyes that were the perfect match for his. Never having experienced this kind of unwavering love and kindness before, he didn't know how to respond. What he wouldn't have given for this man to be at all his academic assemblies over the years or his high school graduation or boot camp.

Joseph Shepherd would have shaped his life differently.

Ryan moved over to clap Joseph on the shoulder and asked, "Sir, are you going to be my first skydiving student?"

Gabe shared an identical look with his grandpa, eyes wide with both eyebrows raised. No way could he picture Joseph Shepherd free-falling from a plane.

"Well, I'm not sure I'm as much of an adrenaline junkie as you fellas are," he started, his eyes shifting between them. "But, you might be able to talk me into it."

"Yes!" Ryan pumped his fist then offered it to Joseph. Eying his outstretched hand, a smile began to curve Joseph's lips. Finally, his fist bumped Ryan's, and a deal was made.

Gabe was blown away by how quickly his life had changed over the last few days. Meeting Holly, owning a business, talking joint business ideas with Ryan, and truly solidifying a relationship with the man who stood before him. A man who had accepted him with his whole heart the moment he'd met Gabe.

His heart was full indeed.

Chapter Twelve

Holly tucked the bottle of champagne under her arm and pushed the doorbell. The pizza box wobbled on her hand when she stepped back. She glanced back at the blowups full and swaying in the wind. His yard was aglow from the lights on his house and bushes. Seeing the train moving around the base of the tree on its track brought a smile to her face. She hoped Gabe's Christmas spirit was at work here.

The door opened and she turned to face it, a wide smile flashing her dimples on her cheeks. Her lips formed an "O" in surprise at seeing Ryan at the door. "Oh, hi."

"But the prettiest sight to see," he sang in a surprisingly deep and rich tone, "is the *Holly* that will be *at* your own front door."

Holly laughed, tilting her head with one eyebrow quirked. "Nice."

"Shut it, Ry." Gabe suddenly appeared and shoved Ryan from the doorway. "Hi, come in." He reached out and took the pizza box and the bottle from her hands. She followed him across the threshold and into the kitchen. "What's this?" he asked setting both items on the island.

"I wanted to celebrate your big win today. Thank you for texting me earlier to let me know it was official." She leaned against the island and added, "I was dangling from Rebecca's roof when I got it."

Gabe's eyes widened over that admission.

"I was safe, I promise."

Gabe looked at Ryan and said, "She decorated Rebecca Ingraham's house today."

"I love her!" Ryan's dark brown eyes lit up. "I just downloaded her new album yesterday. Was she there?"

Holly shook her head. She'd been hoping to meet her. "No, but her agent met us and let us on the property. It was pretty cool. I hope she loves it."

"I can't imagine her not loving it." Ryan jerked a thumb over his shoulder at Gabe who was bringing plates and glasses to the island. "Unless she's a grumpy ass like him."

Gabe grumbled, "Hey."

Ryan turned to Gabe and asked, "So does that new office of yours have a couch?"

"No, no, you don't have to go," Holly said, waving a hand at him. "I'm not staying. I just wanted to come over and celebrate. I have to leave in a few minutes." Holly accepted the plate with a steamy slice of pizza. "Thank you." Holly took a bite and wiped her mouth with the napkin Ryan handed her. "I thought of a fun idea. How about you do a flyover on Christmas Eve? The whole town will be there in the park. You could pull a banner advertising your new business. What do you think?"

Gabe grabbed the bottle next and worked the cork free. Holly jumped when it popped even though she was prepared for it. "That's an interesting idea. I'll have to think about it. I don't know anyone who does banners. But I'm sure Amos could help me with that. He said he'd love to stay involved in an advisory role."

He held up a glass and she quickly said, "Only a small amount. I'm headed to the park soon. And nobody likes a tipsy elf."

Ryan and Gabe shared a look, both men seeming to be biting their lips. She realized how that sounded and laughed, shaking her head. "Okay, fellas, keeping it rated G for the kiddos."

Holly watched as Ryan downed a slice of pizza in two bites. Impressive. Gabe ate at a more normal speed and held his glass up. Holly grabbed hers and did the same. Ryan joined them and Gabe spoke. "To beginning new adventures." Gabe kept his eyes directly on hers as they all tapped glasses. She could drink to that. Starting a new adventure with him was exactly what she wanted for Christmas.

***

Holly waved to the kids going by on the train that ran on a track around the inside perimeter of the park. The engineer tooted the horn and waved back to her.

She loved seeing how happy the kids were. Laughing and carefree, not feeling an ounce of the stressful holiday pressure like some adults might be feeling at this point so close to Christmas.

Holly was one of those people who had most of her Christmas shopping done by Halloween. Not liking the feeling of being rushed or the desperation to find the right item at the last minute, she tended to gather things throughout the year that she thought would make the receiver happy. Having such a large family she'd always been a planner.

Snow crunched beneath her feet as she walked along the path around the park. She was happy to see that the side of the hill where sledding had been set up this year was still packed with snow. Luckily it faced north, so it stayed in shadow most of the day. There was more snow in the forecast in a couple days. She loved having a white Christmas. As kids they'd always wished for it. And boy did they have some epic snowball fights with other kids in their neighborhood. They built incredible forts and defended them until frostbite was imminent.

"Holly, why are you here so early?"

Holly turned to see her mom coming her way down the path, her Santa hat lit with glowing bulbs. Carrying a cup of steaming hot chocolate, her rosy-cheeked face held her ever-present smile with twin dimples. Holly smiled in return and hugged her, sinking in, drawing in the familiar scent of her mom's shampoo.

"There are only three days left until Christmas," Holly exclaimed, pulling back. "I just wanted to make sure things were in order and I wasn't needed to—"

Her mom cut her off, taking hold of her hand. "Honey, you work too hard and do too much. You need to take a break."

Holly glanced away, suddenly nervous. But she reminded herself about her pep talk from a few nights ago. She needed to say no to more things, whittling down her schedule, finding more time for herself. Figuring this was as good a time as any, she pulled in a deep breath and looked into bright blue eyes that matched her own. "Mom, this is my last season as an elf."

Her mom squeezed her fingers. "Good. It's time, honey. Past time. You need to take time for yourself and do things that make you happy."

Holly felt a flush creep up past her turtleneck, heating her cheeks. Flashing her dimples, she couldn't help but share what had most recently made her happy.

The PG version, of course.

"Well, Mom, I have some news to share. I met someone. And he's making me very happy."

"Oh, that's wonderful," her mom squealed, wrapping her up in another hug, rocking her back and forth in her excitement. "I'm so happy for you. I can't wait to meet him."

***

"I can't believe you dragged me down here again," Gabe grumbled. "I thought we were going out for a beer."

Ryan slapped him on the back. "And we will. Definitely. Just thought you might want to see more of what's going on down here. I saw they had games. We didn't get to play any games last time. You know how competitive I am."

Outside he was grumbling, but inside Gabe was excited to catch a glimpse of Holly. This Christmas madness was starting to grow on him. Even hearing the constant music wasn't making him twitch anymore. He'd forgotten to ask her how long her shift was. Maybe she could join them after.

He could have a hot chocolate ready for her.

"I see you. I know who you're looking for," Ryan said in a sing-song voice.

Gabe just shook his head at his friend in response. The grin and eyeroll were part of the package. He couldn't count how many times he'd had the same response to Ryan over the last ten years.

They'd just entered the park, and he couldn't believe the crowd. It was Friday night so he could see why there might be so many people here. The town was small, but its citizens were close-knit and active. He'd witnessed it on the 4th of July, then again on Labor Day and Veterans Day. This town liked to put on parades and fireworks celebrations.

Now that he was going to be a permanent resident, he needed to think about participating more. He wasn't going to join the chamber of commerce or run for mayor or anything, just maybe join his grandpa some weekday mornings for coffee at the diner so he could be in on the hustle and bustle of town.

"There she is."

Gabe looked up from his musings and zeroed in on where Ryan pointed. There she was. In all her elf glory. Her G-rated elf self. Gabe couldn't wait until Christmas to see the naughty side of her.

Glancing at his watch, he figured she'd be up on the gazebo right now. But she was on the path heading towards them. Her eyes downcast, her expression a little sad.

"Hey! Holly," Gabe called out when they got close to her.

Her head whipped up, her gaze taking a brief second to focus on him. Then her dimples flashed and his heart lurched. Damn she was beautiful.

"Hey. What are you guys doing here?" She laughed. "Y'all look like you're looking for trouble."

"Hey, I can't help it, that's how I always look," Ryan quipped. "I thought you were ho-ho-ho-ing tonight."

Holly shook her head and dropped her gaze. "I was kicked out of Santa's Village."

Ryan's eyes widened. "Ohh, what did you do? Did you actually get tipsy from that half-glass of champagne?"

Holly chuckled and smiled up at Gabe. "No, my mom told me to skip my shift tonight. I happened to tell her that this was my last season as an elf, and she told me to go have fun instead of feeling the pull of family obligations."

Gabe was happy for her. She'd told him she felt stretched thin this year and needed to let something go. "Well, let's go then. I see there's sledding over there. Have you been?" Wrapping an arm around her, he nuzzled his mouth against her temple.

"I'm not dressed for it."

Gabe immediately took off his puffer jacket and slipped it on her. "I can't do anything for your legs, but maybe some hot chocolate will help warm you up."

"I'll go grab us some and meet you by the hill." Ryan took off in the direction of the food trucks.

"Hope you don't mind him tagging along. It was his idea to come hang out here again," Gabe explained, wrapping his arm around her back as they turned in the direction of the sledding hill. "Wanted to play some games. He grew up in Miami, so snow and a true winter are foreign to him."

Holly nodded. "Of course. I felt lost not being up there with Santa. So running into you guys was perfect." They maneuvered around the crowd and got in line, turning to watch the others before them sled down the hill. "I forgot to ask earlier. Did you go for a celebratory flight after the deal was done?"

"We did. Ryan, me and," he paused to look down at her, "Joseph."

Holly turned a surprised look his way. Yep, he still felt that way too. "Joseph? Oh, I'm so glad he was there to share in that celebration with you."

"Me too. I was shocked to be honest."

Holly put her gloved hand on his chest, right over his heart. "That's because you've not had enough experience with a loving family that supports each other. That's there for each other to celebrate the wins and comfort you through the trials."

Gabe nodded, his eyes focused in the distance. No, he hadn't. But he wanted that. Maybe it was time to take that next step and start calling him Grandpa to his face, not just in his mind. By showing up today, Joseph proved that he obviously wanted that role in Gabe's life.

Holly leaned her head against his shoulder and wrapped her arms around his back. Gabe tucked her head under his chin and pulled her close. He loved how perfectly they fit together. "Are you warm enough?"

"Enough," she said into the fabric of his thick sweater. Luckily, he'd chosen this one since his outer layer was currently keeping Holly warm enough. Gabe moved his hands up and down her back, stroking vigorously to help generate heat under the down layer.

"This'll help." Ryan stepped up beside them in line. He held out a steaming cup to Holly. She accepted it with both hands and brought it to her mouth, blowing lightly across the top before taking a sip. Gabe's gut tightened when she moaned and rolled her eyes back in her head.

Gabe turned to Ryan and asked, "What? None for me?"

For a brief moment Ryan's eyes widened like he'd goofed. But he quickly recovered and smiled. "Nah, you don't like hot chocolate."

"Just messing with you, man." Gabe stepped forward when the line ahead of them moved. Holly and Ryan followed.

"Does your town go all out like this every year?"

Holly nodded and swallowed a sip before answering. "Yes, every year. With a name like Tinsel, it's expected." Holly glanced around and waved back to a woman standing off to the side watching the sledders. "We added a couple new things this year. Sledding is one. And the Christmas Tree maze is new. It looks fun," she added.

"We will definitely go there next," Ryan declared, tipping back his cup to drain the remainder of his hot chocolate. "I grew up in Miami. It definitely didn't have a cozy, small-town vibe like this one. We celebrated Christmas, just with white sand and palm trees. We did decorate a tree each year and hung up lights on the house, but it wasn't as cool as this." Gabe thought Ryan sounded wistful. If things progressed according to their chat this afternoon and he went into business with Gabe, then Ryan would get to experience this every year.

The line moved and got them closer to being up next. Gabe eyed the sleds that people were using and hoped they were sturdy. When it was their turn, Holly took her last sip and put her cup in the trash can sitting at the fence line. Gabe carried his sled and hers to the edge of the hill. Ryan followed behind with his.

Ryan let out a loud *whoop* and hurtled his body head-first down the slope. Gabe and Holly laughed and took their time getting settled. "Wanna race?" Gabe asked.

Holly looked over, eyeing him from the top of his beanie-covered head to his butt on top of the sled. Then she grinned and pushed off the ground, tipping herself over the edge of the slope. He heard her laughter as she sped up. Gabe used his boots to dig in and followed beside her, catching up easily. Holly noticed and leaned forward trying to gain more momentum. She was still a foot ahead of him. Ryan stood at the bottom of the hill wiping snow off his chest. He must have busted.

"Go, Holly!" Ryan cheered her on, getting in position to see from the side who crossed the finish line first. "Go, Holly!"

Gabe laughed when the foot of Holly's sled crossed the line a hair before his did. He pulled the rope and directed his sled to keep it from running into the others gathered at the bottom of the hill. Holly let out a shriek and he felt her sled plow into his back. She must have tried to steer and overcorrected. Gabe toppled off his sled, landing on his shoulder and hip in the wet snow. Holly rolled off hers and ungracefully landed across his body. Together they made the shape of an X. Gabe let out a grunt on impact. Then about choked on his laughter when she slugged him in the chest.

"Haha, funny." Holly tried to push off him and rise, but Gabe grabbed her and pulled her forward until she lay on top of him, covering him from head to toe. "Oh, I like this landing spot much better," she whispered as she lowered her head for a kiss. Gabe closed his eyes and felt her melt into him. If only they were alone. Pulling back from the kiss, he had to blink his eyes a couple times to clear the haze that had come over them. He wouldn't call them tears, but happiness might be leaking out of his eyes. Her beautiful blues glimmered in the bright lights, totally focused on his eyes.

"I love you, Holly."

Gabe completely surprised himself when those words slipped out. With wide eyes and a rounded mouth, he figured he'd surprised Holly as well. She opened her lips to speak but closed them with a hesitant snap.

"Sorry, that just came out," he explained. Heat instantly flooded his body the second the words passed his lips. He wondered if she could feel his heart trying to thump its way out of his chest. Gabe wiped some snow out of her hair, realizing she must have lost her elf hat somewhere. "I've never said that to anyone before. But I'm confident that love is what I'm feeling. It's the strongest emotion I've ever felt."

"No need to apologize," Holly said, her voice thick with emotion. "I like that you shared your feelings with me."

"You don't have to say it back," he quickly added. "It's crazy soon after meeting and you might not—"

"Feel the same way," she finished for him. Her dimples flashed at him when her lips curved up. "But I do feel the same way, Gabe. It *is* crazy soon. But sometimes when you meet someone you just click. And we've definitely clicked, babe."

Feathering his fingers through her hair, Gabe pulled her down for another kiss. His lips open and consuming. He wanted Holly just like this but naked and in his bed. Not on a bed of snow.

His ears finally registered a throat-clearing sound near his head. Loud and repetitive.

Gabe released her lips, sighing against her mouth, his forehead pressed lightly against hers. "Sounds like we have company."

"Yeah, probably not the best place to make out," she giggled, placing a fast kiss against his lips before pushing off him. Gabe saw that Ryan reached out to help her stand. Then Gabe took his turn. Ryan pulled him to standing with one hand. He felt every inch of snow that was trying to seep through his clothing. He would freeze soon if he didn't get changed, but it had totally been worth it.

Gabe wrapped his arms around her back and kissed her temple, whispering against her ear, "I'm one lucky sonofabitch."

Chapter Thirteen

Holly tried to hide her yawn behind her coffee cup. It was the third one that escaped in the last thirty minutes. She was in the final planning meeting with the town council group responsible for the Christmas Eve extravaganza in the park. The crowd was about thirty strong, with most people just representing a group or organization contributing to this event. It was the biggest event that the town puts on. And that's saying something because they go all out for all the holidays.

Her mom and dad were in attendance as well. She had come in with one minute to spare before the start of the meeting, so she was sitting in the back of the auditorium.

Thoughts of last night kept dragging her attention away from the mayor speaking about the list of vendors. Stolen kisses in the Christmas tree maze, high fives when beating Ryan at snowball target tosses, then later that night wrapped in each other's arms beneath the glow of the fireplace. Their shared passion, their declarations of love solidified in those heartfelt, steamy moments. Holly was amazed at how fast her feelings for him manifested. She'd never experienced a love like this before. This over-whelming, this consuming, that her whole heart was bursting with love for him.

"Holly, did you have something you wanted to add?"

Her friend sitting next to her bumped her arm with her elbow. "Hey. Snap out of it. They're calling for you."

Holly dropped her feet off the back of the chair in front of her, her boots clonking on the hardwood floor and sat up straight. Her eyes snapped to the leader of the town council who was now speaking. When had that happened? Boy, she must have been lost in her sexy day-dreams for a while now.

"Yes, hi."

"Holly, come on up and share with the plan-ning committee the idea you came up with and have already started executing the plan for."

Holly set her coffee mug on the floor beside her chair, then rose to her feet and made her way to the front. Her mom gave her hand a squeeze when she passed by. Her heart pound-ed extra hard as she ascended the steps to the stage.

Turning to face the crowd she found her mom's smiling face to ground herself. She'd never had a public speaking role. Shyness wasn't necessarily something she dealt with, but being in front of a crowd always brought a certain level of stress. Holly cleared her throat and announced, "I've made contact with the local children's home in the neighboring town of Kelly. There are twenty-three children who are in foster care but haven't been placed in homes yet. I have met with the director and we came up with a plan for the children to get to experience the magic of Christmas."

She turned her smile on her dad. "With the help of my dad, the big guy himself, and Debbie and Mike Patronas who bring the reindeer to town each year, we are going to surprise the kids with a visit from Santa riding in on a sleigh filled with gifts." She heard several *oohs* and *ahhs*. "The children will be treated to dinner at Ralph's Diner, then will arrive at the park just in time for their surprise. We have received some amazing donations in such a short time so that each child will get two presents. So thank you all for your help with this. It's going to be a magical experience."

A round of applause started in the back and worked its way forward. The crowd's enthusiasm warmed Holly's heart. She'd been inspired by Gabe and his past. She knew that she had to do something, and hoped that it would become a tradition each Christmas.

She would see to it.

"Thank you, Holly!" the town council chairperson called out. "Your generosity of spirit and time made this happen. We will definitely vote to make this a reoccurring event each year. This town is full of heart and overflowing with the Christmas spirit."

"Oh, one more thing," Holly added with a dimpled smile because she was about to say the name of the man she loved out loud. "Gabriel Shepherd has recently bought out Amos Tucker's pilot licensing business. He will be doing a flyover during the event pulling a banner advertising his business."

"That's a great idea," the mayor said. "Maybe we can do that each year. Even during the parades for our other events. People can pay him to advertise their businesses."

Others spoke up offering more ideas. Holly was happy that she was getting Gabe some potential business connections. Pretty soon she'd have to invite him to one of these meetings, now that he had permanent ties to Tinsel, Tennessee.

***

"Sir, you make a mighty fine steak," Ryan said, leaning back in his chair at Joseph's kitchen table, rubbing his stomach.

"There's another one available. Gabe told me to cook extra because you eat like a tank, I believe he said." Joseph grinned at Gabe and winked.

"That I do. I have a high metabolism," Ryan explained and happily reached for the remaining steak on the platter with his fork.

"Thank you, Joseph, this was a delicious meal." Gabe took another bite of steak then washed it down with a sip of beer. Joseph had invited them over for dinner, wanting to get to know Ryan more. Ryan being the talker that he was helped Joseph out by telling him more than he probably wanted to know. But his grandpa just sat back in his chair and laughed over story after story that Ryan shared. There was an easy camaraderie between Ryan and his grandpa.

Gabe felt a little envious. He was comfortable with him and had shared a lot about himself. But he was holding back, keeping the bad stuff locked up tight so Joseph didn't know who he'd been as a kid. The kid who'd struggled, who'd taken care of his mom more often than she'd taken care of him, who'd gone hungry sometimes.

But maybe that period of time didn't matter so much. Maybe he didn't ever have to share about that part of himself. Maybe his grandpa cared more about who he was today than who he'd been when his mom was still alive.

Joseph had told him stories about his mother and how she'd been before her mother had died. That she'd been in ballet, sang in the middle school choir and loved to ride her bike. She'd been a carefree child. But when her mother got sick, she'd become withdrawn, sad, unreachable. Then after she'd died, Joseph had tried to comfort her, but she'd already been lost to him by that point. It hadn't been long after they'd buried her mother that she ran away. His grieving heart had broken all over again.

Gabe tuned back in to Ryan telling Joseph about their adventures last night at Santa's Village. "You should try the sledding. It was a blast."

Joseph laughed. "I can't see myself sitting on a sled and going downhill fast without toppling off."

"Then you'd end up just like Gabe and Holly." Ryan turned his grin on Gabe. "Except they decided lying in the snow was the perfect place to make out."

Feeling his face heat up, Gabe tried to hide it behind his napkin, using it to wipe his mouth. Gabe looked over to find his grandpa grinning at him.

"Well, isn't that something? Holly Noelle," Joseph whispered her name. His head tilted and his knowing gaze pinned Gabe in his seat. "I have something I want to give you."

Gabe glanced at Ryan when Joseph tossed his napkin on the table and left the room. Ryan shrugged his shoulders. Gabe wondered what it could be as he stood and carried his empty plate and glass to the sink. Then he started to pick up the serving dishes.

Ryan stood with his plate. "I'll get the rest of this. You go see what he's got for you."

Gabe set the items back down and dried his hands on his napkin. "Thanks, Ry."

Gabe passed through the kitchen doorway into the living room. He'd been here many times but felt like he spotted something new each time. Old family photos lined the mantel and the bookcases. Photos of his mother when she was a baby all the way up until she was sixteen. Photos of them together as a family. Gabe was drawn to one photo in particular. It was of his mother around age fifteen wearing a dress standing next to a boy in a suit. It looked like it was probably taken before they went to a school dance. The smile on her face was brighter than he ever saw. Her eyes were so luminescent. She just looked happy. They'd had happy times together, just not often.

"That was her boyfriend in ninth grade, Kyle Strickland. The photo was snapped right before they were going to their homecoming dance." Joseph paused beside Gabe. He could feel the sadness oozing from him. "That was how I have always remembered her. The happy-go-lucky angel that her mother and I were blessed with."

Gabe reached an arm out, hesitant at first, then grew bolder. Wrapping his arm around Joseph's shoulders, he squeezed, offering him comfort. Gabe felt a pinch in his gut but breathed through it, taking an extra moment before he said, "Would it be okay if I call you grandpa?"

Joseph's arm slid around Gabe's waist and pulled him closer. "I'd be honored."

Moving to stand in front of him, Gabe put both arms around his grandpa. They hugged for a long time. Gabe thought they both needed this. The connection. The comfort. The acceptance.

Joseph pulled back and asked Gabe to sit. They moved to the couch and Gabe turned to see what Joseph carried in his hand. It was a small black box.

"This was my wife's—your grandmother's—engagement ring. It is for you to do whatever you wish with it."

Gabe couldn't believe it. He didn't know what to say. He just stared at his grandpa.

"That's customary sometimes in the south. To pass on family heirlooms like this. I couldn't bear to get rid of it after she died. But I want you to have it. To give it to a woman who holds your heart."

Gabe thought of Holly. She definitely held his heart in her hands. Suddenly a plan started to take shape in his mind. "Thank you, Grandpa."

Joseph's eyes started to shimmer. "I never thought I would get to hear that. I'm so lucky that I found you, Gabe."

He had to swallow hard before he could speak. "I'm happy that you did too. But I'm the lucky one," he countered. "I get to see pieces of my mom's past that I never would have if you hadn't reached out. I would have never known the friendship, the kindness, and the love of a grandfather. I would have never known what I've been missing out on my whole life."

"I love you, son. You're a fine young man. A Marine. An aviator. So strong, capable, confident. You are responsible for being who you are." Joseph reached over and took hold of Gabe's hand. "You had to grow up in some unpleasant conditions which only helped build your character from an early age. The Marines fine-tuned who you were always meant to be. I'm just glad I get to share some years with you now."

Gabe's throat had constricted with emotion the second his grandpa said "I love you." He swallowed hard and blinked his shiny eyes before saying, "Having me in your life—and Ryan—is going to keep you young."

"I look forward to it," Joseph said wiping a tear off his cheek. "I think I might look forward to skydiving too."

"I heard that!" Ryan called out from the kitchen. "You're gonna be my first customer, Grandpa!"

Gabe and Joseph shared a smile, both of their eyes wet with happiness.

Chapter Fourteen

The kids have finished their dinner and will be headed to the park in five minutes.

Holly couldn't help the sizzle of excitement that raced through her belly when she read the text. The butterflies must be doing backflips in there. She immediately sent a text to her dad alerting him on the kids' progress. Eve was riding with him on the sleigh. They were just down the street on the opposite side of the park, ready and waiting for their signal. Holly was to alert them once the kids were seated on the bleachers set up beside the gazebo.

Townspeople milled around Santa's Village. Shouts of joy could be heard from the ice rink and the games section. Holly stood with her mom near the gazebo. Both were sipping hot chocolate. Ms. Tessie had extra helpers tonight because the kids were all going to be treated to hot chocolate and doughnuts from the local bakery for dessert. She'd made an extra-large batch and would ladle it up as soon as the presents were opened.

"Holly, I'm so proud of you for putting this all together," her mom said, gently bumping shoulders with her. "This is just what this night needed."

"Thank you, Mom. It was Gabe who inspired me. When he was young and in foster care, he never experienced Christmas. I don't want any child to miss out on the joys, the surprises, the wonder that we experienced growing up."

"That's very admirable of you. What did Gabe say when you told him about it?"

"He was speechless. Honored. Said it helped his Christmas spirit grow even more." Holly hid her flush behind her cup and looked out toward the crowd of people. They might have been talking about this while they were in the shower together, and that was not a picture she wanted to paint for her mom. Luckily, her mom changed the subject.

"What time is Gabe scheduled to fly over?"

Holly glanced at her phone. "In about forty-five minutes."

"All right, I think those kiddos are about to head our way. Let's go greet them," her mom said leading the way to the bleachers. Holly sent that text signal to her dad and Eve.

Kids of all ages, sporting newly purchased winter coats, hats, gloves and boots trudged happily through the snow. A few babies wrapped up tight in winter gear and fleece blankets were carried by caregivers. Seeing all these kids made her heart hurt. Knowing they didn't have the stable childhood that she had. Knowing that there was so much uncertainty and sadness in their young lives. She hoped tonight gave them so much joy and wonderful memories to hold in their hearts.

"Hello, kids, Merry Christmas!" she called out as she moved to stand in front of them. "Did y'all enjoy your dinner at Ralph's tonight?"

She heard a collective "yes" and paused to wave at a little girl who looked about four who stood up and waved at her. "That's wonderful! Well, we have a surprise for you tonight. Let's listen really hard. Raise your hand when you hear bells."

Holly turned to look out in the direction all the children were facing. In the distance the faint sound of sleigh bells could be heard. Behind her, squeals of delight. "Me! Me! I hear bells!" one girl shouted. Holly looked back at the bleachers and saw a sea of smiles and several hands in the air. The jingling of bells grew louder as the sleigh approached. A collective gasp when Santa and his elf came into view warmed her heart. The reindeer looked stunning, decked out with red scarves and ornaments dangling from their antlers.

"Santa!!! He's here!"

"Oh, wow!"

"Can we talk to him?"

Holly took a deep breath hoping to hold her tears of joy at bay.

Her heart was full.

She wished Gabe was here by her side for this. "Yes, you'll get to talk to him. You'll get to see the reindeer up close and even sit in the sleigh with Santa!"

The children broke into happy cheers. She was so thankful that her mom was close by snapping pics and had Caroline videoing the children's reactions so she could share it later with all the donors who helped make this night special for these children.

"Ho, ho, ho, Merry Christmas!" Santa called out as he brought the reindeer to a stop in front of the bleachers. The reindeer snuffled and snorted, steam drifting from their mouths, their hooves stomping in the snow.

The children's home director organized the children and brought them over a couple at a time. Debbie and Mike helped the children who wanted to pet the reindeer. A couple brave souls even fed them straw from a nearby wagon.

Eve hopped down from the sleigh and helped the children up onto the bench to sit next to Santa. He put his arm around them and accepted their hugs of delight. He chatted with each child, wishing them well and then handed them two presents each. The children's faces were priceless. Their happiness palpable.

The last ones to visit Santa were the three babies. Her dad looked so precious cuddling those little ones. A tug in her uterus had her picturing little babies with green eyes and dimples.

Holly looked around at the controlled chaos and felt her heart grow inside her chest. Children ran around throwing foam planes into the air; others were hugging dolls. She was so happy to see all of this come together so well and so quickly. The town council chairperson came up beside her and bumped her shoulder. "You done good, kid."

Holly blushed. "Thank you, ma'am. I'm just so glad that everything worked seamlessly."

"That was because of the excellent planning on your part. You should think about running for town council."

Holly groaned inwardly. Being stretched thin already she wasn't looking to add anything to her plate. At least not now. "I'll keep that in mind."

Holly's mom finished taking pics of the last baby in her dad's arms and strolled over to them. "It's almost time for Gabe to fly over, isn't it?"

"Oh!" Holly had gotten so caught up in the precious moments happening before her that she almost forgot. She pulled her phone out and saw that she'd missed a text from him. "He said ETA ten minutes, but that was five minutes ago."

Holly excused herself from the chairperson and moved over to a clearing. Caroline and Bella came to stand beside her, both chattering about how much fun that was and how sweet the children were.

"Holly, you're a real do-gooder," Bella said, entwining her arm with Holly's.

"You make that sound like it's a bad thing, B," Caroline said, frowning at their youngest sister.

Bella shrugged. "I don't mean it that way. Holly does so much for other people. Tonight was just one example."

"It was a beautiful experience for those kiddos," Caroline said. "It warmed my heart hearing all their cheers and seeing their eyes light up when Dad and Eve rode up."

Holly listened to her sisters with only one ear. Her other tuned to the sky overhead, listening for the plane's engine. Looking up, Holly spotted the thick cloud cover. She hoped it was safe to fly tonight. She really needed to learn about aviation so she could feel more comfortable with him up in the air.

Glancing around her, she realized that flakes were beginning to fall. Her eyes tracked several larger flakes then caught on the man standing off to her left. Joseph Shepherd. He offered her a smile and a raised-hand wave. Holly returned his grin. "Hello, Mr. Shepherd! Gabe is five minutes out," she called out, waving to him before returning her hand to her pocket. She'd accidentally forgotten her gloves this evening.

Holly was so happy for Gabe that he had Joseph in his life. He needed family, and Joseph was a good one to have. He and her grandfather were like bosom buddies, meeting for coffee every morning at Ralph's Diner and alternating hosting a card game that she'd heard could get pretty intense.

Suddenly an engine could be heard overhead, the snow clouds reverberating the sound back to the ground. Holly focused her attention to the east knowing that Gabe planned to fly across the park, east to west.

Her heart began to thump hard, for no other reason than the man she loved was coming within sight. She fumbled with her phone in her pocket.

"I've got it," Caroline told her, her phone already out and aimed at the sky. "You just watch your man."

The plane came into view. The sign being pulled behind it had lights making up letters, but it was still too far away to know what it said. A smile curved her lips thinking about how competent her man was.

And how could she possibly be thinking about him as "her man"?

Already.

So soon.

She was so focused on the cockpit, trying to see inside that she wasn't prepared for when her sister Bella started smacking her arm, yelling, "OMG!! Holly!!"

Holly had to blink her eyes, thinking she must be mistaken at the words she saw forming before her eyes when the plane flew overhead across the park.

"Holly!!" Now Caroline was tugging on her arm, her phone still pointed at the sky, trailing the plane and its banner.

Holly felt her mouth drop open as her brain finally caught up to her eyes.

In lights above, the sign read: *Holly—Light Up My World—Marry Me?*

Holly's hands slowly lifted to her face, covering her mouth. "Oh..." That was unexpected. Her hearing clouded over, her heartbeat thumping so loudly that it blocked all sound. She felt like she was suddenly underwater.

Tears covered her eyes and she rapidly blinked them away, not wanting to block her view for even a second. In moments the plane was out of sight.

"Holly? What? Who?" Bella yelled, slapping her arm again. "Sister, you've been holding out on us."

Holly chuckled, feeling the laugh bubbling up from deep inside.

The butterflies now had the zoomies.

"Holly." A deep voice penetrated her clouded hearing. Her sisters squealed, then Caroline pulled Bella back, giving Holly space, as she slowly turned, disbelieving.

How is he here?

But there he was. Gabe stood beside his grandpa, the biggest grin on his handsome face. He looked so confident, so real. But how could he be there when he was supposed to be flying the plane? A furrow formed between her brows.

Her expression must have conveyed her question.

"Ryan," he explained, tilting his chin up.

Ahh, that made sense. "Tricky."

Gabe's boots crunched on the snow as he moved toward her with sure steps, no hesitation, no faltering. His hands were tucked in the pockets of his puffer jacket, and he wore jeans that molded to his fit thighs.

All the sounds of the crowd around them faded when he was touching-close. Strong hands curled around her arms, then slid down to lace his fingers with hers. His heat instantly warmed her cold skin.

She couldn't blink. Couldn't look away from his mesmerizing eyes. She didn't want to miss a second of this magical moment. Her Christmas wish was coming true, right before her eyes.

She and Gabe were starring in their own real-life Hallmark Channel movie. If there wasn't one already in the works like their story, then someone needed to get on it and write the screenplay. Because this was perfect.

"Holly," Gabe started, "did you see the banner?"

Holly pulled her lower lip into her mouth, pressing down with her teeth, and nodded. "I did. Light up your world, huh? I thought I already did that, and you weren't too pleased."

"I wasn't ready for it then." Gabe released her right hand and lifted his, moving the hair off her face, tucking it behind her ear. Sending her dangling snowman earring spinning. Reaching out with a fingertip, he swiped a snowflake off the end of her nose. "But I am now. I want it for the rest of my life. I want you, Holly," he whispered, bringing her left hand up to his lips to kiss her fingers. His steamy breath sent a shiver up her arm. The intensity in his gaze sent those butterflies into zoomies once again. Holly's eyes were hot with emotion, tears collecting along her lower eyelids.

"You are my forever." The tone of his voice radiated throughout her heart as he spoke each word with conviction. "It all starts with you, with us, with this magical moment."

Those beautiful words broke the dam and sent tears rolling down her cheeks.

"My forever starts with you, Holly." She'd been so lost in his gaze that she didn't notice he had a ring in his hand. The diamond winked in the glow of the lights strung overhead as he held it up to her. "I have you. I have Joseph. I have Ryan," he added with a mock eyeroll which brought a grin to her face. She knew he loved Ryan like a brother. "I have everything that I could ask for."

Holly wiggled the fingers on her left hand, giving him the hint that he needed to get on with it already. Her hand was still snug in his and he brought it up to his lips once more before sliding the ring onto her finger. Holly's eyes followed the action. Tingles radiated out from where the ring slid over her skin. "Marry me, Holly?"

Holly felt her heart melting in her chest. Lifting her eyes off the most beautiful diamond ring she'd ever seen, she focused back on his lustrous green gaze. "I want forever with you, Gabe. I told you sometimes people just click. And you and I most certainly click."

"My life clicked into place the moment I met you, Holly. Falling in love with you made me want to leave the past behind and focus on the present. And hope for a future," he added, resting his forehead against hers. "I want one with you, Holly."

"Yes, Gabe, I want that too." Holly wrapped her arms around his neck and pushed up on her tiptoes. "Yes, I'll marry you. Our forever starts now."

Gabe pulled her close and pressed his lips against hers. She kept it simple and sweet for the public that had gathered around and were now cheering and clapping. Settling back on her boots, Holly looked into a beautiful pair of eyes that she felt lucky to get to admire forever.

"That was a pretty impressive trick you played on me."

Gabe's grin was priceless. "It was the perfect way to end the holiday season. Now I'll have even more to look forward to each Christmas." Gabe leaned into her, his lips grazing her ear. "The present I'm most looking forward to this Christmas," he whispered, "is unwrapping your naughty-list elf lingerie beneath the Christmas tree."

Holly couldn't think of a better present or a better way to spend this Christmas of firsts. She hoped that each year brought them a new adventure. One that they could explore together, forever.

About the author

Ivy Beck enjoys writing Contemporary Romance and Romantic Suspense with emotion and humor woven throughout. Her former life was spent teaching marine science along coastal Alabama. She switched to raising kids and editing for several New York Times bestsellers a few years ago. The kiddos are older now giving her time to let her creative mind wander. Ivy loves her boys, her pets and spending time outside. She loves kayaking and hiking. The water and the woods are her happy places. She lives in south Alabama with her husband, two sons, two dogs and one cat, and spends most of her day being a mom taxi. Which, surprisingly, is a really good place to think about the next chapter of her current WIP!

* 9 7 9 8 3 3 0 6 4 7 3 9 2 *